"So tell me, *cara mia,* what is to stop me *persuading* you to return what belongs to me?"

The glitter in Vito's eyes had intensified. Rachel's breathing had quickened and adrenaline was coursing through her bloodstream.

But she knew she was deceiving herself.

She could feel her body responding to his presence; feel every nerve leap to quivering life.

It mortified her. She had to damp it down hard, because she knew, with a terrible, sickening sense of doom, that she would feel this way about Vito Farneste for the rest of her life. She could never stop the tide of desire, of longing, of *wanting,* pulsing through her whenever she was near him. She was in thrall to him, and it was a captivity she could never escape....

Julia James

HIS WEDDING RING
OF REVENGE

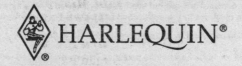

TORONTO • NEW YORK • LONDON
AMSTERDAM • PARIS • SYDNEY • HAMBURG
STOCKHOLM • ATHENS • TOKYO • MILAN • MADRID
PRAGUE • WARSAW • BUDAPEST • AUCKLAND

ISBN 0-373-12476-7

HIS WEDDING RING OF REVENGE

First North American Publication 2005.

www.eHarlequin.com

Printed in U.S.A.

CHAPTER ONE

COOL tranquil fountains jetted softly over the rounded stones, the water pooling, crystal clear, over polished granite. A tiny spout of wind gusted off the tall building and one of the gentle plumes of water wavered slightly, a minute spray of invisible droplets misting over Rachel as she walked past.

It felt cool to her skin.

And that was what she had to be. Cool, calm and composed. Not a trace of emotion. She was here to conduct a business deal. That was all.

Because if she thought about what she was about to do in any other light then—

No! Don't think. Don't feel. That way you can get through this.

And, above all, don't remember...

A switch was thrown in her brain, cutting off the line of thought.

Another mist of water flickered over her skin.

She took in the serene tranquillity of the cunningly engineered water feature that graced the entrance to the gleaming new office block. As befitted the UK headquarters of one of Europe's largest and most successful industrial conglomerates, Farneste Industriale, it was the most prestigious of all the blocks on this swanky new business park—situated on the edge of one of London's oldest villages, Chiswick, conveniently placed for the M4 motorway and Heathrow Airport.

She kept on walking, her high heels lifting her hips and making her sway elegantly in her expensively tailored suit.

She had sat very carefully in the taxi on her way here, making sure she did not crush the lavender skirt or snag her expensive sheer stockings.

She wanted to look—immaculate.

It had taken her over two hours to get ready. Two hours of washing and styling her hair, delicately applying perfect make-up and nail varnish, carefully donning silky underwear, sheerest stockings, soft cream camisole, and then finally gliding the narrow pencil skirt over her slender hips and slipping her arms into the satin-lined, scoop-necked waisted jacket that subtly accentuated the swell of her breasts and the flatness of her stomach.

She had slid her feet into soft Italian leather shoes, in exactly the same shade as the suit, as was the matching leather clutch handbag she carried, and her outfit was complete.

It had taken her over two weeks to find it. After combing every upmarket department store and boutique from Chelsea to Knightsbridge, Bond Street to Kensington. It had to be exactly right.

After all, the person she had to impress had demanding standards. Exceptionally demanding.

She should know.

She had once failed them. Dismally. Abjectly. Humiliatingly.

She must not fail this time.

And now, as she walked up to the huge double doors that opened automatically at her approach, she promised that she would not. This time, she knew, she could hold her head high against any female she was compared with.

True, some might prefer petite brunettes or voluptuous, flashy redheads to her lean, chic blondeness, but of her style—if you liked that style—she was perfect.

Soignée. That was what her mother would have called it, approvingly.

Emotion clutched at Rachel's heart. She subdued it instantly. Feelings of any kind would be fatal in this encounter. If she had any hope of succeeding she must be calm, confident and totally composed.

She was here to do business. Nothing more.

Absently, as she started to walk across the huge, echoing entrance lobby, she heard the automatic doors hiss softly shut behind her.

As if she were a prisoner.

A tiny prickle of apprehension snaked down her spine. She subdued it.

She was not a prisoner. She was not even a hostage.

She was here to propose a transaction, nothing more, which would have a favourable outcome for both parties.

Perfectly straightforward. So much so that no emotion whatsoever would be required of either of the participating parties.

She went on walking across the vast marbled floor, up to the huge semicircular reception floor in the middle, behind which towered another cleverly designed water feature: a wall of water so smooth it hardly seemed to be flowing at all.

Cool air wafted from the wall of water, freshening the artifice of air-conditioning that eased around the whole building.

She halted in front of the smartly dressed receptionist, who looked at her with polite enquiry.

'I am here to see Mr Farneste,' said Rachel.

She spoke in a composed voice, placing her clutch handbag on the wide reception desk surface that acted like a barricade around the woman she had just spoken to.

'Your name, please?' replied the receptionist, reaching for an appointment book.

'Rachel Vaile,' she answered, her voice unwavering.

The receptionist frowned.

'I'm sorry, Ms Vaile, there doesn't seem to be an entry for you.'

Rachel was undismayed. 'If you phone his office and give my name, you will find he will see me,' she said, with calm assurance.

The receptionist looked at her uncertainly. Rachel knew why, and gave an inward, caustic smile.

You think I'm one of his mistresses, don't you? And you don't know what to do if I am. Am I on his current list? Or will he have given his PA orders not to put me through if I phone or, even worse, show up in person?

The caustic smile turned bitter. She knew the routine. Oh, yes, she certainly knew the routine.

'One moment, please,' said the receptionist, and picked up the phone.

Rachel's lips pressed together. She would be checking with his PA, as a good Farneste employee would always do.

'Mrs Walters? I have a Ms Rachel Vaile in Reception. I'm afraid I can't see an appointment in the book.'

There was a moment's silence.

Then, 'Very well. Thank you, Mrs Walters.' From the expression on her face Rachel could tell what she had been instructed to do—dispose of her.

She was about to put the phone down. Calmly, Rachel intercepted the movement and took the receiver from her. The receptionist made a startled objection, but Rachel paid her no attention.

'Mrs Walters? This is Rachel Vaile. Please inform Mr Farneste that I am in Reception. Tell him...' she paused only for a hair's breadth of time '...that I am in a position to offer him something that he considers very precious to him. Thank you so much. Oh, and Mrs Walters? You should tell him straight away. In three minutes' time I will be out of the building, and the offer will be withdrawn. Good day.'

She handed the receiver back to the receptionist, who was looking at her speechlessly.

'I'll wait over there,' she told the woman coolly. She glanced at her watch, picked up her clutch handbag, and went across to the island of white leather sofas surrounding a huge circular table on which the day's papers were arranged with punishing neatness.

She picked up a copy of *The Times* and started to read the front page.

Precisely two minutes and fifty seconds after she had handed the phone back to the receptionist, a phone at the desk rang. Rachel turned the page of the newspaper and continued to read.

Thirty seconds later the receptionist was standing beside her.

'Mrs Walters will meet you on the Executive Floor, Ms Vaile,' she told Rachel.

There was a note in her voice that Rachel would have been deaf not to recognise.

Astonishment.

The lift glided her upwards. Bronzed walls reflected her in infinite regression, increasingly shadowy. As the doors opened a neatly dressed middle-aged woman stepped forward. Her face was bland.

'Ms Vaile?'

Rachel nodded, face expressionless.

'If you would come this way please...'

She led the way forward along a wide expanse of space, carpeted in cream and interspersed with pieces of large, abstract statuary. It was imposing, impressive. Designed to be intimidating. Intimidating to impudent interlopers such as herself, who had no business being here.

But Rachel was here to do business.

Nothing more.

And nothing less.

As they gained the far side of the atrial space she could see another reception desk, with two young women working there, both exceptionally beautiful. Rachel's mouth tightened, but her expression did not alter. She was led past the two receptionists, aware of them looking at her as she walked by, and then past the office that was clearly Mrs Walters's own. She was taken straight up to a large pair of chestnut wood double doors.

Mrs Walters knocked discreetly, and opened one of them.

'Ms Vaile, Mr Farneste,' she announced.

Rachel walked in.

Not a trace of emotion was in her face.

He was exactly the same. Seven years had not altered him. He was, as he would remain all his days, the most beautiful man she had ever seen.

Beauty, she thought absently. Such a strange word to apply to a man. Yet it was the only one that fitted Vito Farneste.

The sable hair, the superbly chiselled face, the high, sculpted cheekbones, the fine line of his nose, the edged plane of his jaw.

And his mouth. Perfect, like an angel's. But not an angel of light.

An angel of sin.

Temptation made visible.

He leant back in his black leather chair, perfectly still. One hand rested on the surface of the ebony desk. Against that blackness it seemed pale, yet its olive hue was dark against the pristine white of his cuff, the golden gleam of his watch.

The other hand rested on the leather arm of his chair, elbow crooked slightly, long fingers splayed, motionless.

He did not get to his feet.

Rachel heard the soft click of the door and realised that Mrs Walters had performed her duty to a T.

Eyes surveyed her, dark and expressionless, with lashes so long that they lay on his cheek. Impassive. Dispassionate.

He did not speak.

But in that silence she heard in her head, as if time had dissolved, the very first words he had ever spoken to her.

Eleven years ago. She had been fourteen. Just fourteen.

Tall. Gawky. Plain.

Like a half-grown colt.

It had been the school summer holidays. The first week She had been supposed to go and stay for a fortnight with a schoolfriend, but on the last day of term Jenny had come down with a belated childhood infection and her parents had rescinded the invitation. The school had informed Rachel's mother, and at the last moment a ticket had been sent, flying her out to Italy.

Rachel hadn't wanted to go. She'd known her mother didn't want her around. Hadn't wanted her around ever since she'd been taken up by Enrico Farneste and had moved to Italy to be as close to him as she could. Now her mother only ever saw her for a week or so every school holiday, in a London hotel paid for by Enrico. Rachel knew Arlene was always glad when the visit was over and she could get back to Enrico.

But this holiday, with nowhere else to go, Rachel had ended up in Italy all the same.

The villa Enrico had installed her mother in was beautiful, nestled into the cliffside above a fashionable seaside village on the Ligurian coast, within easy reach of Turin, where the Farneste factories were. Never having seen the Mediterranean before, Rachel had found herself enchanted despite her reluctance to be there, and on that first afternoon, upon being deposited at the villa by the chauffeured car that had met her at the airport, she had wasted no time in running down to the azure-tinted swimming pool on the lower terrace.

Apart from a housekeeper who spoke only Italian the villa had seemed deserted, despite the presence of a sleek red monster of a car in the driveway. Her mother and Enrico, Rachel had assumed, as she glided blissfully through the warm clear water beneath the Mediterranean summer sun, must be out.

But as she'd reached the shallow end of the pool, after a dozen lengths or so, and halted momentarily, one arm hooked over the stone edge of the pool, hair slicked back in a soggy pony-tail over one shoulder, to catch her breath before preparing to turn and head for the deep end again, she had realised the villa was not deserted after all.

Someone had been standing at the top of a short flight of stone steps that led from the upper terrace down to the pool area. Male, late teenage, maybe even twenty, obviously Italian. Very slim. Tall.

For a moment he had gone on standing where he was, unmoving.

Then, slowly, he had begun to walk down the steps.

He'd been wearing cream-coloured chinos, immaculately cut and styled. One hand had been thrust into a pocket, tautening the material across a washboard stomach. A tan leather belt had snaked around his lean hips. An open-necked, cream-coloured shirt had been rolled back slightly at the cuffs, and around his shoulders an oatmeal jumper.

He had descended the steps with an indolent, lethal grace that had stopped the breath in Rachel's lungs.

Her eyes had been dragged from the column of his throat, revealed by the open-necked shirt, and as they'd reached his face she had felt every muscle in her body tense unbearably.

It was the most beautiful face she had ever seen.

Sable hair, feathering slightly over a tanned brow,

sculpted cheekbones, planed jaw and nose, and a mouth…a mouth that made jellyfish squirm inside her stomach.

He'd worn dark glasses, and he'd looked just so cool, so glamorous, as if he'd just stepped out of a scene from a film, or off a poster.

Her stomach had tensed with nervous awareness, making her feel stupid and dazed.

He had stopped at the bottom of the stone steps, about two metres from the edge of the pool. He had looked at her. His dark glasses had veiled his eyes, but she'd suddenly— despite the sporty cut of her swimsuit—felt incredibly exposed.

Had he known she was supposed to be here?

She hadn't had the faintest idea who he was, but she had known instinctively that he was the sort of person who knew who *he* was—and that was someone who could go anywhere he pleased. It wasn't just his breathtaking looks, there'd been a natural, arrogant grace about him that would have elicited instant accommodation to any wish he might have. Especially by females. He was the sort of male girls would just drool over, fight over, play totally, bitchily dirty to get his attention.

With a horrible sort of dawning embarrassment Rachel had realised that, right then, it was *she* who was getting his attention.

And she hadn't liked it.

It hadn't been just that her housemistress's parting warning about the predilections of Italian males towards young females was ringing in her ears. She'd felt self-conscious, horribly so. Because, whoever he was, he'd obviously known he had every right to be there, but, given the unexpectedness of her arrival, he might not have known that she had too. It had also been due to the way he'd looked down at her, his face, what she'd been able to see of it, given that his eyes were veiled, expressionless.

Her costume might have been the world's least glamorous swimwear, but for all that it had moulded her body and exposed her legs and arms, shaping her figure.

She didn't have a very good one; she had known that. Compared with some of her age group she'd been pretty underdeveloped, especially in the bust department, and all the sport she'd played had made her arms muscular. As for her face—well, it was OK-ish, she supposed, but it was pretty ordinary.

For a male like the one who had been staring down at her, 'ordinary' might as well not exist.

She had known exactly what kind of girls he would date. The A-list girls, the ones oozing sex appeal, who looked fabulous every moment of the day. The ones who totally outclassed all the other girls and who knew exactly just how hot they were.

Any other girls could just forget it. Give in. They wouldn't even register on his radar.

All this had gone through her mind in a few scant moments, and she had realised that, since she was *not* an A-list female—even one far too young for him—she wouldn't even exist for him as a member of the female species. So what would it matter if he thought her swimsuit unalluring and her face and figure likewise?

What had mattered, though, was that he might think she was trespassing—or gatecrashing, or something—some tourist chancing it at a deserted posh villa.

He had continued looking down at her, one hand still thrust into his trouser pocket, the other hanging loose, his expression blank and unreadable. Had he been waiting for her to say something? Explain her presence?

Embarrassment had flushed through her. She'd raised a hesitant hand in a sort of wave, or some sign of visual communication. The moment she'd done it she felt a fool. But it had been too late to back off.

'Hi,' she said awkwardly. 'You're probably wondering who I am, but—'

The moment she started speaking she realised she was an even bigger fool. She was speaking English, and it was totally obvious that he was Italian. No English male could *ever* look that svelte, that beautiful...

He cut her short.

'I know exactly who you are,' he said. He spoke in English, completely fluent, his Italian accent doing nothing to soften the flat harshness of his words. 'You're the bastard daughter of my father's whore.'

CHAPTER TWO

ELEVEN years later his voice was just as harsh, just as flat, the Italian accent just as unsoftened.

'So, you've finally decided to cash in your last asset.'

His eyes went on surveying her, completely without expression.

Yet as his unblinking, impassive gaze rested on her she could see, very deep at the back of his eyes, a flash of gold.

Emotion pinpointed her, like a sniper's bullet. And just as deadly.

That flash of gold came only at two moments.

The first was when, as she knew he must be now, he was keeping a leash on that tight, white rage that could lash out with such lethal devastation.

He had done that with the very first words he had ever said to her.

If she'd had any instinct whatsoever for survival then, she knew, with bitter accusation, she would have made sure they were the last words he'd ever spoken to her.

But that stupid, gormless fourteen-year-old had had no such instinct. Only one for encompassing with sure, deadly accuracy her own total ruin.

She felt her nails curve with a minute jerk into the soft leather of her handbag. And that was why she knew about the other moment when that flash of gold in his eyes came.

Out of nowhere, after the last seven years of ruthless, relentless suppression of any feeling to do with the man who was now sitting there, not three metres away from her, came a bolt of memory that she would have given her right hand not to be remembering now, here.

No! *No!*

She forced the memory aside.

You are here for one thing only. One purpose. One aim. A single business transaction.

She sharpened the focus of her gaze on him.

Feel nothing. Remember nothing.

He sat there, waiting for her to pitch. He knew she would pitch. It was what he had let her in to do. It was the sole justification for her continued existence as a data field in his mind. She didn't exist otherwise.

Did I ever exist?

The question came, treacherous, pointless.

No, she had never existed for him. Not her, not Rachel Vaile.

Not the person she was—her soul, her mind, her personality, her likes and dislikes—nothing, about the person she was existed for him.

Not even my body existed for him.

I thought it did, in my naïve stupidity. I thought that at least my body existed.

But it hadn't. Only one thing had mattered to him about her.

Over the wastes of eleven long years his words echoed in her mind.

'I know exactly who you are—you're the bastard daughter of my father's whore...'

That was who she was to Vito Farneste. It was all she ever had been. All she ever would be.

And then, into the welling seepage of old, old bitterness, a new thought came. One that made her vicious with sudden satisfaction.

She *would* be more to Vito Farneste.

If he wanted to do business with her.

Her shoulders pulled back with a minute, almost invisible

straightening. Her gaze rested on his blank, impassive face, no trace of emotion, none whatsoever, in her eyes.

And she pitched.

'There are conditions,' she began.

Vito held himself still. Every fibre, every muscle in his body was under total control.

It was essential.

If he had not imposed such ruthless control over his body it would have hurled itself from his chair, thrust past his desk and his hands would have curved around the shoulders of the woman who dared, *dared* to stand there offering him *conditions*, and he would have shaken her, and shaken her and shaken—

His mind slammed down. Even allowing himself the image was lethal. It might take over and become reality.

Instead, he merely continued sitting there, quite motionless.

Surveying her.

Rachel Vaile.

Crawling out of the woodwork after seven years.

Although in an outfit like that she wouldn't be soiling her knees or laddering her stockings by crawling anywhere.

His eyes took in every detail.

The hair, the suit, the nails, the accessories.

He ran up a price tag for the total look.

Five hundred pounds? Easily—another few hundred if you added the shoes and the handbag.

Where was she getting the money from?

The answer knifed through his head, making the question obsolete.

Other men.

Well… He eased the sudden, inexplicable tensing of his shoulders as the answer formed in his mind. She certainly had the right genes for it.

A family profession…

He went on surveying her.

Not that she needed the family link to trade on. Her looks had matured at last. She was, he thought dispassionately, at the very peak of her physical appeal now. And she certainly knew how to package herself.

The knifeblade went through him again, but he ignored it. It was as incomprehensible as it was irrelevant.

He went back to studying her physical appeal.

She didn't flaunt that racehorse leanness, that ash-blonde fall of hair, those wide, haunting eyes and the tender mouth…

No!

A blade sliced down over his mind.

Fine. She looked superb. Resplendent.

Fantastic.

So what? Now move on. Her looks had nothing to do with him.

Nothing about Rachel Vaile had anything to do with him. They never had and they never would.

Only one thing about Rachel Vaile was of any concern to him.

The price she was intending to exact.

Sitting back calmly in his chair, he merely allowed the sweep of his lashes to lower minutely over his eyes.

'And your price is—?'

There was contempt in his voice. He didn't even bother to hide it.

Did something move in her face? He couldn't tell. But she answered in the same voice as she had first spoken. 'I didn't say "price". I said "conditions".'

That spurt of rage iced through him again. She had the *insolence* to come here, forcing his hand like this—

Because she was forcing it, all right! For three years— *three years*—he had tried by every means he could to get back what was his—*his!* His lawyers had been useless. Imbeciles! A gift, they had told him, was a gift. It conferred legal title on the recipient. And his father had, after all, given his mistress many gifts. Valuable ones. Expensive ones. Including jewellery…

Vito had cut off their prating with an oath.

'*Dio mio*, do you seriously mean to compare the trashy baubles he gave his whore with the piece she *stole* from him?'

His lawyers had looked even more spineless and useless.

'It would be difficult to assert that she did so in a court of law, Signor Farneste,' one of them had ventured uneasily.

Vito had rounded on him mercilessly. '*Cretino!* Of course she stole it! My father was no fool! He didn't even give her the villa! Why the hell would he have given her something worth even more?'

'Perhaps as a token of…ah…appreciation…er…*instead* of the…ah…villa?'

Vito had stilled. A closed, deadly look had come over his face. In a soft, lethal voice that had made the lawyer step back automatically, he had said. 'You think so, do you? Tell me, what man gives his mistress his wife's wedding present? What man gives his whore the Farneste emeralds?'

The Farneste emeralds.

Rachel could still see them now. It had been nine months ago. Her mother had insisted on Rachel accompanying her to the bank. Demanded she go into a little room, set aside, where a bank official had brought a sealed parcel to them and placed it on a table, together with a form. They had been left alone, and her mother had pulled off the restraining string around the boxlike parcel, unwrapping the brown paper to reveal a jewel box. Not a very grand one, just one that opened up, revealing a shallow upper layer and a deeper

one beneath. Her mother had only glanced at the top layer,
lifting it up out of the way to expose the lower one.

And Rachel had gasped. She hadn't been able to help it.

A river of green fire had flashed in the light. Her mother
had lifted it out and sat back. A look had settled on her face.
An expression of extreme satisfaction. She'd let the jewels
flow through her hands and given a deep, contented sigh.

'It's incredible!' Rachel breathed.

Her mother smiled.

'Yes,' she said. 'And it's mine.'

There was a strange note in her voice. Not just pleasure
at owning such a treasure. More than that. And Rachel recognised what it was.

Triumph.

A sense of foreboding started to sound in her.

'The Farneste emeralds,' said her mother. 'And they're
mine.'

Then a strange, haunted expression came into her eyes.
She looked at Rachel.

'They'll be yours. Your inheritance.'

Vito leant back in his chair behind the vast desk that befitted
the chairman and chief executive of Farneste Industriale.
The company was only three generations old, but the
Farneste family went back a lot further than that. The
Farnestes had been merchant princes at the time of the
Renaissance, and though the family's fortunes had fluctu-
ated wildly over the intervening centuries, now, thanks to
Enrico's shrewd, hard and brilliant brain—a throwback to
his Quattrocento ancestor—the Farneste fortune was riding
high again. Vito's task was merely to steer Farneste
Industriale into the expanding global economy of the
twenty-first century.

But though the Farnestes looked forward, Vito had not
forgotten the past. The ancient past—which had brought the

Farneste emeralds into existence in the eighteenth century—
and the recent past—which had scarred his youth.

Thanks to Arlene Graham's poisonous presence in his
father's life.

A poison he had not yet quite drawn. The very last drop
of that vicious venom had yet to be extracted.

And Arlene's daughter was here, offering him the chance
to draw it.

'Conditions?' he said expressionlessly. 'By this you mean
exemption from prosecution for theft.'

Vito's voice was flat. Unarguable.

Rachel shifted her weight slightly. The tension in her
spine was making her back ache.

But when she replied her voice was as flat as his.

'Had there been justification for prosecution you would
have gone ahead years ago,' she replied. 'The conditions I
require to be met are quite different.'

She watched Vito's face for his reaction. There was none.
Not even anger at being reminded of how completely im-
potent he was to use the force of the law to return what he
considered his. He would have done so if he could. She
knew that. Without the slightest hesitation Vito Farneste
would have used the full force of the law to regain his pos-
sessions.

After all—her eyes shadowed—he had done it once already.

What Vito Farneste wanted, Vito Farneste got.

He made sure of it.

Whatever it was and whoever it was.

For whatever reason.

She stared at him. Stared at the man who sat there, who
had nearly—so very, very nearly—destroyed her.

I was young. I was stupid. I was gullible.

She was none of those things now.

And Vito Farneste meant nothing to her. Just as she meant nothing to him. Had always meant nothing to him.

Now, only one person meant anything to her. It had come very late, but it had come. And it was for that reason she was here, standing in front of Vito Farneste, offering him the one thing he wanted from her—the only thing of any value to him.

But you were never of value to him—never! Not once, at any time! You were nothing more than a fool, to be used.

His eyes were dark, so very dark. Like the night.

For a second so brief she wanted to believe she had only imagined it, a pain went through her that was searing, agony.

*For I have sworn thee fair, and thought thee bright
Who art as black as hell, as dark as night...*

The lines from Shakespeare's bitter sonnet tore at her.

With a strength she pulled out of grief, she forced her mind away.

Vito Farneste wanted different things now from what he had wanted once, when she had been that young, stupid, gullible fool. Now what he wanted was in her possession.

But, unlike the last thing he had wanted from her, this time she would extract something in return.

Not money. Money was no use to her.

What she wanted was something quite, quite different.

Vito's eyes had narrowed. But they remained utterly without expression. She matched hers to his.

'Well?' he demanded.

His gaze bored into hers.

She felt them do so as if they were a physical force,

drilling through her. She took a breath—quick and sharp and shallow.

'It's very simple,' she told him. 'I want you to marry me.'

For a second there was total and absolute silence. Then, like the lash of a whip, he started to laugh.

It cut the flesh from her bones, flayed the skin from her body.

Scornful, contemptuous laughter.

She watched his head thrown back, his mouth widen, indenting lines from his nose to the edges of his lips.

Then he cut the laughter short.

With dark, poisonous venom in his eyes he leant forward.

'In your dreams,' he sneered.

His mocking voice sheered through her. Forcing her to acknowledge the truth of what he said.

Once, marrying Vito Farneste would have been a dream come true.

But that was in another lifetime. When she had been a different person.

Yes, so naïve I should have had a warning sign on me!

But there had been no warning. No warning of just how mortally dangerous Vito Farneste could be to her.

After that first, horrible encounter by the pool, when she was fourteen, she'd never thought she would see him again. Her mother, arriving back after a long lunch with Enrico, had been furious to discover Vito had turned up at the villa. Vito's father hadn't seemed pleased either.

Rachel had stayed down by the pool even after she'd heard the car arriving and assumed it was her mother and Enrico coming back. But she hadn't been able to block out the angry exchange of deep voices echoing down from the house, culminating in the throaty roar of that red beast tearing away up the precipitous coast road. After a while her mother had come in search of her, clipping down the steps in high heels and looking tense and distracted. There had been two spots of colour on her cheeks, visible beneath the perfect make-up she wore. At thirty-four her mother could easily have passed for a woman nearly ten years younger, but today she showed her age.

'Are you all right, Mum?' Rachel had been moved to ask.

Her mother had given an impatient sound in her throat. 'Vito has been here, spreading his usual discord! Enrico is angry, naturally, and that just makes for a difficult situation.'

'Who's Vito?' Rachel asked, though she was pretty sure she knew just who her mother was referring to.

'Enrico's son. He's driven here, quite unnecessarily, to inform his father that his mother has taken off for her mountain chalet with one of her so-called nervous attacks! Does Vito seriously think Enrico is going to rush after her? He's only been here two days —that boy has absolutely no idea how hard his father works!' Her mouth tightened. 'The only thing Vito knows is how to spend money and live the *dolce vita* in Rome! The original Latin playboy!' Her eyes suddenly sharpened. 'Did you see him?' she demanded. 'Before Enrico and I came back?'

To her chagrin, Rachel felt the colour flush through her face.

'He…he walked past the pool,' she confessed, in a mumbled voice.

Her mother's face hardened. 'Well, at least he won't be back now. He's gone off to hold his mother's perpetually swooning hand. It's quite ridiculous the fuss he makes over her!'

Was that defensiveness in her mother's voice, or just accusation? Rachel wondered. Whichever it was, it just made her long to be a million miles away.

She remained of that opinion for the rest of her stay at the villa. She did her very best to stay out of the way, heading down to the tiny private beach below the villa to swim in the sea, or sunbathing by the pool with a book.

Her mother and Enrico seemed to spend most of their time out and about, and she was glad. She felt no easier in Enrico's company than in her mother's. He seemed to be a remote figure, middle-aged and heavily built, someone around whom the whole household revolved—including, primarily, her mother.

Rachel hated seeing them together. Up till now she had accepted their relationship. It had lasted over six years, ever since Enrico Farneste, attending a conference in Brighton, had walked into the expensive boutique her mother ran in the fashionable Lanes to buy something for his current mistress and decided that Arlene Graham would make him a much better one. Rachel had been packed off, first to her mother's elderly widowed aunt and then to an expensive boarding-school, to get her out of the way, and her mother had been whisked off to Italy.

Rachel had known her mother had become the mistress of Enrico Farneste, head of the giant Farneste Industriale. That it was his luxurious villa she lived in, his yacht she took her holidays on, his gilded world she moved in. And she had known, too, that it was thanks to Enrico Farneste that she went to her exclusive boarding-school, that Auntie Jean now lived in a nice bungalow outside Brighton, not a council flat, and that when she stayed with her mother in London it was Enrico Farneste who ended up paying for the hotel, and supplying the money her mother spent.

Her mother was untroubled by the irregularity of the liaison.

'On the Continent these things are understood,' she had told Rachel, in her crisp voice. Her vowels had completely lost their flattened, lower-class origins, and her spoken English now was almost as good as her expensively educated daughter's. 'In a Catholic country a wife can never be divorced, so men have no choice but to stay married. It's a perfectly acceptable arrangement, and no one thinks anything of it. Just as no one,' she added offhandedly, 'thinks anything of the fact that your father and I were not married.'

She had sounded so convincing that Rachel had believed her.

Until Enrico's son had ripped that illusion from her with a handful of casually vicious words. As ugly as they were true.

Surely to God that should have been warning enough?

But it hadn't been.

The ugliness of the words had not been enough to make her forget the beauty of the man who had delivered them. From that day onwards Rachel had hidden a shameful secret—that in her adolescent heart every male who ever came her way, whether real or on screen, was compared to Vito Farneste. Even as the years passed, and the routine of school dominated, still, in the dark recesses of her secret mind, she knew she could never expunge the image, burnt on her retina by the bright Italian sun, of that figure walking down the steps with lithe, leashed grace, like a dark, beautiful young god.

She had told no one—Vito Farneste had remained a secret sin.

It was one she was to pay for bitterly.

Was still paying for. In dreams that had turned into a nightmare.

A nightmare that was the dark, deadly sting of Vito Farneste's eyes as she told him her conditions for relinquishing the Farneste emeralds.

He sat back in his chair.

'Get real,' he said, his voice soft. Soft as blood.

Rachel could feel the scorn, the derision, lashing out at her like the fine, cruel tip of a whip across the broad desk. She saw him reach out a long-fingered hand and pull open one of the drawers of the desk, take out a leather cheque-book case. He flicked it open, and picked up a gold pen, sliding off the top and holding it over a cheque.

'Cash,' he said. 'That's the currency for women like you and your mother. Hard cash.' His eyes narrowed, and Rachel could feel the leashed fury lashing within. 'But don't even think of trying to bleed me. You can have a million euros in exchange for the emeralds. Not a cent more. Take it or leave it.'

He was starting to write. Assured, decisive, the black ink flowing smoothly across the blank spaces of the cheque.

'No sale.'

Rachel's voice was controlled. Very controlled. It had to be.

Vito didn't even pause in writing, just went on, scrawling 'one million euros' in the required space.

'You didn't hear me, did you?' Rachel said. Was her voice less controlled? No—she would not allow it to be. Must not allow it. Too much depended on her keeping her control total. Absolute. Unbreakable.

Vito glanced up, his look corrosive. 'I heard you make a joke in such poor taste I would not have thought even *you* could stoop so low.'

He went back to completing the cheque, signing it with his dark, flowing hand. He tore the page from the cheque-book and pushed it across the desk towards her.

'I've dated it three days from today. Bring me the emeralds tomorrow, and then you can cash the cheque.'

She didn't even look at it. Instead, in a tight, rigid voice, she said, 'It was no joke. If you want the emeralds back, you marry me. That's all. Take it or leave it.'

She could not resist throwing back his own words to her. It helped, however minutely, to ease by a fraction the tension racking her so tightly she thought she might snap at any moment.

Vito set down his pen. It was a slow, deliberate movement. Then, in a movement equally slow, equally deliberate, he leaned forward again.

'I would rather,' he spelt out, his voice low, lethal, 'take a toad as a wife than you.'

His eyes rested on her. Dark. Deriding.

A dull stain of colour seeped out along her cheekbones.

'I'm not suggesting a real marriage.' She tried to inject scorn into her voice, but it didn't seem to come out that way. She could feel the colour spreading now, staining her cheeks. 'I simply want your ring on my finger for a limited duration.'

A pang struck her, stabbing with a pain she should have got accustomed to but hadn't. Couldn't.

'Six months—no longer.'

The tightness in her voice was unbearable, crushing her larynx so she could hardly speak. The pain stabbed at her again.

She tried to stare him down, match his cold, levelling gaze with one of her own.

'I have already given you my answer. Do you add selective hearing to all your other...flaws?' was Vito's response. 'Including, of course, stupidity. Do you imagine I would ever, under any circumstances, marry *you*?'

Her face was so tense it ached, all the way across her jaw, up through the bones in her skull. Her spine was stiff with the strain of holding herself upright.

'I know what you think of me, Vito— I don't need it spelt out.'

A slashing, hostile smile flashed across his face. Utterly devoid of humour.

'Then, if you know that, even more do I question your sanity in coming here like this. Daring to try and sell back to me what was never your bitch of a mother's to take!'

Emotion—deep, agonised—twisted in Rachel's face.

'Don't speak of her like that!' Her words spat at him.

Vito's face darkened, as if night had closed over him.

'Your mother got her greedy, grasping claws into my father and wouldn't let go! She made my mother's life a nonstop misery!'

His words, his voice, cut at her like a knife. Rachel closed her eyes against it. How could she deny what he had said? How could she argue back against what he had thrown at her? And yet to hear her mother spoken of in such terms gutted her. A vision of how she had last seen Arlene seared into her mind, and she had to open her eyes again to banish it. But she could not banish the shaft of anguish that went with the vision.

She raised her hand in a sharp, sweeping movement, as if to brush away the feelings ripping through her.

With monumental effort she fought back to take control of her emotions, to keep this conversation where it had to be—at the level of business, nothing more. Where Vito Farneste would gain something he wanted and so would she.

'This is irrelevant,' she said dismissively. 'The sole issue is whether you want the Farneste emeralds back again—on the terms I've just set out. I want your ring on my finger. For no more than a few months—' she fought to keep her voice steady as she spoke '—and that's all. You can have your precious emeralds back on our wedding day. No cash will be necessary.'

She bit out the final sentence.

Vito stared at her. His expression was veiled. And suddenly the way he was looking at her was far, far worse than when his eyes had been dark with fury, his face cold with disgust.

She felt her heart start to quicken, her stomach plunge as though she'd just swallowed an ice-cube.

'Why?' he asked quietly, but there was no softness in his

voice, just a low, disturbing shimmer of menace. 'Why?' he asked again.

His shoulders eased into the soft leather curve of his executive chair and it swung slightly at the redistribution of weight. His eyes never left her face.

She shifted uneasily. What was going on? Why was he looking at her like that?

She tightened her jaw.

'Why what? Why don't I want money for the emeralds?'

'No. Why do you imagine that I would entertain, even for a nanosecond, your...proposal?'

His voice was still quiet, but it withered the flesh on her body.

'Because,' she answered, through gritted teeth, 'you want the emeralds back. And this is the only way you're going to get them.'

Something flashed in his eyes. In a single fluid movement he was on his feet.

His hand flew up.

'*Basta!* This idiocy has gone far enough! I am prepared to buy back the emeralds in cash—but I am not prepared to have my time wasted a second longer with this farce! So either take the cheque or get out!'

She was reeling from the force of his anger. Her fingers dug into the soft leather of her handbag.

'If I walk now you'll *never* get your precious emeralds back!'

She tried to hurl her words at him, but they came out shaking.

'Never is a long time,' he retorted caustically. 'At some point you'll sell them—just to realise their value. And if you don't sell them to me, what do I care? I'll buy them from whoever you sell them to.'

'My mother will never sell them!' An image of the way Arlene had let the green jewels run through her fingers, gloating with triumph over her possession of them, shot through her mind. 'Never!'

'Then you can bury them in her grave with her!'

Rachel's face whitened, draining of blood. Faintness drummed in her ears.

'You bastard,' she whispered.

His face stayed unrelenting, like unyielding marble. 'No—that's you. Remember?'

It finished her. Finished her totally.

Numb, she turned on her heel, walking back towards the closed double doors that seemed suddenly to be a hundred metres away. The urge to run, to get out, was overwhelming. Only at the door did she find one last vestige of courage. She took the handle, steadying herself.

Then she turned. Her face was totally blank.

'May you rot in hell, Vito Farneste!'

She swung back, yanking open the double doors, and walked out. She just made it inside the lift before her legs all but buckled beneath her, and she had to sag against the bronzed wall for support.

As the lift plunged downwards, so did her heart.

She had blown it. Totally blown it. Her wild, stupid, *insane* idea had failed utterly, miserably.

Despair filled her, and in its wake the floodgates to grief opened yet again, drowning her.

In his office, Vito stood for one long, last moment, his face rigid. Fury so overwhelming he thought it would burst through tore at him, but he leashed it tight, with rigid control.

How *dared* she come here! Stroll into his office and coolly, insolently, lay down conditions for the return of his own property?

And such conditions...

His eyes narrowed with cold, disbelieving rage.

Had she really imagined that he would pay the slightest consideration to what she demanded? Could she really be that insane? Walking in, out of the blue, three years after he'd finally torn Arlene Graham's grasping claws from the Farneste coffers, and thinking that he might actually consider, let alone accept paying such a price for the purloined Farneste emeralds?

Out of what sordid hole had she crawled, anyway? And why now? Were times hard for the pair of them these days? He'd made sure Arlene Graham had taken the minimum of booty with her when he'd despatched her after his father had died, but a woman like her would have squirrelled away funds for years. Other than sending his useless pack of lawyers to try and extract the one trophy she had managed to carry off, he'd let Arlene Graham rot, glad that he'd finally got her out of Italy. Where she'd gone he neither knew nor cared. If she'd taken another protector he'd have been surprised—her youth had gone and her market rate was all but zero.

Another thought seared across his mind.

Had she turned her daughter to the same trade? Leeching off rich men in exchange for sleeping with them? She was certainly dressed as if a rich man had paid for her appearance…

Even at the thought something stabbed at him. So brief that he dismissed it. Instead he found himself jabbing at the intercom to his PA.

'The woman who left my office just now. Have her followed.'

CHAPTER THREE

RACHEL turned the key in the lock and let herself into her flat. She felt overwhelmed with emotion, shaking in the aftermath of her encounter with Vito Farneste.

It had been worse, far worse than she had imagined it could be—even though she had been dreading it ever since the realisation that she would have to go and confront him had gelled inside her all those weeks ago.

She collapsed down on the bed. It sagged ominously under her weight. But she took no notice. The grim condition of the rented bedsit she lived in was of no concern to her—she had ceased to notice its noisome condition some time ago, and if she missed her small but beautifully decorated one-bedroom flat in the old Victorian house in a leafy inner London suburb, she did not regret its sale by an iota. It had had to go, and go it had. And that was that.

Only one thing concerned her now—had concerned her for the last five gut-churning weeks.

Getting Vito Farneste to marry her.

Had she really thought she had a chance of succeeding? She might as well have tried to scale Everest on her hands and knees! She stared bleakly ahead of her, every excruciating moment of that ghastly scene playing itself inside her head like an unstoppable CD.

Her stomach writhed as if it were full of sea snakes, and her hands, she realised, were still clenched tightly around her handbag. Forcibly she made herself unclench them, and tossed the bag on the bed's shabby coverlet. She glanced down at the threadbare carpet.

It had all been pointless. The whole sorry, stupid expedition! The idiotic, no-hope, ludicrous plan! How could she possibly have thought it would succeed? That Vito Farneste would actually consider going along with her proposal to get his precious emeralds back? Agree to anything so absurd, so insane as going through any kind of marriage ceremony with her? However temporary, however limited.

Not even getting back the Farneste emeralds was worth such a sacrifice on his part.

I must have been mad even to consider it...

No, not mad, she thought, her eyes screwing shut in anguish. Just desperate.

Desperate enough to do anything, *anything* to make Arlene happy...

Pain ate at her. Like a huge, engulfing pool it flooded over her. Washing through every pore of her body. She could not stop it—did not even try to these days. Because if she did, it didn't work, simply hit her again, over and over.

Getting to her feet again, she reached to pick up her handbag and extract her mobile phone. The number she knew off by heart, and dialled it automatically. When it answered, her words were automatic as well.

'Hello. This is Arlene Graham's daughter. How is she?'

She waited while the appropriate records were checked, and the same carefully neutral phrase came back to her. Rachel nodded, murmuring her thanks, and disconnected.

Stable. No change. As well as can be expected. Comfortable.

The familiar litany drilled through her head. None of it sufficient to hide the one word that was the truth about her mother.

Dying.

Depression sank over her like a heavy weight, pressing down on her so that she felt slow and cumbersome as she moved around the cramped bedsit, carefully proceeding to take off her expensive, extravagant outfit and smooth it carefully inside the curtained-off hanging space which was the closest the accommodation got to providing a wardrobe.

As she eased the beautiful fabric off another emotion penetrated her cawl of depression. Bitterness that she had wasted so much scarce money on such a pointless expenditure. She might as well have saved it for all the good it had done! Had she really thought that looking the part would help persuade Vito Farneste to accept her ludicrous conditions?

How could it have? Making her his wife—on whatever terms imaginable—was anathema to him, whatever clothes she was wearing!

Get real, he had sneered at her, and he was right. She'd been indulging in a pathetic fantasy, thinking the Farneste emeralds might be a sufficient inducement to go along with her absurd plan.

Again in her mind she heard his contemptuous, angry words cutting her idiotic fantasy into tiny shreds!

Well, it *was* an idiotic fantasy…the whole thing—emeralds or not!

Just how many times does Vito Farneste have to say vile things to you before you learn your lesson about him?

If she'd been smart, the first insult he'd thrown at her when she was fourteen would have been the last! If she'd been more worldly-wise she'd never have given him the benefit of the doubt again.

But she hadn't been smart, she thought savagely. She'd been stupid—criminally, culpably stupid. Indulging herself in an idiotic, ridiculous fairytale.

She tried to stop herself, but it was no good. Like a sweeping, drowning tide memory rushed through her, taking her shakingly, shudderingly back into the past that was like a curse over her life still, all these years later.

Eighteen.

She'd been eighteen.

Such a dangerous age. An age for dreams.

For fairytales.

Her school exams had been over, and the senior class had been allowed two weeks away from school in the summer term as a reward. Her friends Jenny and Zara had whisked her away with them, gleefully informing her that they were going to spend the fortnight in Rome, at Jenny's father's company flat. Rachel had been apprehensive—although she'd been one of the oldest girls in her year she'd known that she was the least worldly-wise—but excited as well.

She hadn't told her mother—anyway, Arlene was cruising with Enrico in his yacht off the French Riviera, so her last postcard had said.

After years of being an exemplary pupil at the strict boarding-school restlessness had swept through her, a yearning for something more than studying and sport and music lessons. A longing for excitement. Adventure.

Romance.

Cold broke down her spine as memory washed over her. *Romance?*

She'd been yearning for romance—but what she had found was something quite, quite different…

She felt her fingers clench.

If I just hadn't gone to Rome. If I hadn't gone to that party the night we arrived. If Vito Farneste hadn't gone. If, if, if…

But she had gone. Dressed up in one of Jenny's evening outfits that showed off so much bare flesh she'd been shocked by it, her face and hair done by Zara so that a golden waterfall had cascaded down her bare back, her eyes huge, her mouth lush.

A totally different Rachel Vaile from the boring school-girl she had always been.

She'd thought she was so sophisticated, so mature, so *grown-up*...

But she'd been like a kid playing games. Games she hadn't even known she was playing.

If I just hadn't gone to that party...

But she had gone, and so, by malign chance, had Vito Farneste. And he had taken his opportunity, handed to him on a plate by a stupid, gullible eighteen-year-old.

Such a vulnerable age.

Against Vito Farneste, at eighteen, she'd had no defences whatsoever.

Most pitiable of all, she hadn't even wanted any.

Her mouth twisted and tightened.

It had been like taking candy from a baby.

All he'd had to do was look at her, that beautiful, sinful mouth smiling at her, his dark eyes washing over her, telling her with his sweeping, long-lashed gaze that she was pleasing to him.

He'd spent that whole party by her side, and he had been the only person in the room for her. Her whole being had focused on him.

She'd recognised him immediately, and frozen, but miraculously he hadn't seemed to recognise her. She'd known that four years on she must look very different from that briefly glimpsed, scathingly dismissed gawky fourteen-year-old in a swimsuit. Moreover, she'd still borne her father's name, not her mother's—and had he ever even known her first name? She'd wondered whether she should tell him who she was, but as the evening had worn on she'd known she could not. Could not bear to risk him dismissing her as cruelly as he had done four years earlier.

He had been like a dream come true. A secret fantasy made real.

He'd whisked her away from the party as it had got rowdier, and driven her around Rome by night in a pow-

erful, open-topped Italian thoroughbred of a car. And she'd
sat, gazing round at the beauty and excitement of the Eternal
City, entranced by the Spanish Steps—so crowded with
tourists, whatever the hour—then the Via Corso and the
Pantheon. They'd driven along to the glistening white wedding cake of the Victor Emanuel monument, and then
through the ancient Roman Forum to sweep past the sinister
mass of the dreaded Coliseum.

But it hadn't just been Rome that had captivated her.

Her hungry gaze had been as much for Vito Farneste,
disbelieving that he was fantasy made flesh—here, now, beside her.

She'd assumed, when he'd finally dropped her off at
Jenny's apartment after midnight, that she would never see
him again, but he'd turned up the next day, after breakfast,
and whisked her off again to see Rome by day.

Jenny and Zara, as thrilled for her as she was herself, had
done her up to the nines again, and once more she had had
the bliss of seeing Vito Farneste smiling down at her, knowing she was pleasing to his eye despite her youth, her
Englishness and her obvious lack of worldly-wise sophisti-
cation.

It had been like a fairytale. Two, beautiful, exquisite, wonderful, gorgeous weeks of having Vito all to herself, during
which she had basked like a flower beneath the sun. She'd
floated three feet off the ground, it seemed, as Vito had
showed her Rome and the lovely, rolling summer countryside
of Lazio, with its pine forests and cooling lakes, and the coast
and the seaside. Everything had been touched with magic—
gazing awestruck, neck cricked, at Michelangelo's Sistine
Chapel ceiling, wandering around the shady avenues of the
Borghese Gardens, watching the children at play and avoiding their madly pedalled go-karts, and the mandatory tourist
ritual of throwing a coin, backwards over her shoulder, as

tradition demanded, into the majestic Trevi Fountain. As she had turned, her return to Rome guaranteed, Vito's arm had come around her shoulder, guiding her through the press of jostling tourists who'd flocked around the edge of the Fountain, cameras flashing, guides expounding, a polyglot of different languages.

The feel of his arm around her had made her almost faint with joy. He'd paused at a nearby *gelataria*, and she'd hovered, delicious with indecision, over the myriad flavours to choose from. Then they'd strolled along, cornet in hand, back towards the Via Corso, across the busy shopping street into the Centro Storico to seek out the glory of the Pantheon.

He'd told her about Rome—all the tourist things, the history things, the modern, gossipy things—smiling at her, laughing with her, and she'd been enthralled, enchanted.

Blinded. Completely blinded.

Completely unable to see what he'd been doing.

There had been a clue she should have seen—a massive clue, totally obvious with hindsight. But not at the time. Not to her—not poor, stupid, little inexperienced eighteen-year-old her.

In all their time together he had barely touched her. Nothing beyond that arm around her shoulder at the Trevi Fountain, or an accidental brushing of fingers when he'd handed her an ice-cream, or the touching of her arm as he'd pointed something out in the Roman Forum.

But nothing else. Nothing else at all.

Until that last fatal night.

Anguish pierced her. Roughly she drew the shabby curtain across the wardrobe alcove and went into the tiny kitchenette, hardly more than a cupboard, to run water for the kettle.

She didn't want to remember! She didn't want to remember that night. That night—the last one she was to spend in Rome—when, instead of taking her back to Jenny's father's apartment, as he always had done every night, after a last coffee in one of the old piazzas, he'd taken her instead to an elegant eighteenth-century building which housed the baroque splendour of the Farneste apartment.

Where, with all the skill and experience of the consummate Italian playboy lover, Vito Farneste had seduced her.

She could feel her eyes sting, pain buckle through her.

It had been an effortless seduction. She had gone into his arms—his bed—rapturously, breathlessly, adoringly. So, so willingly. Her mouth melting under the kisses with which he had dissolved her frail, hopeless resistance to him.

But what eighteen-year-old girl could have resisted Vito Farneste? Could have resisted that lean, svelte body, that beautiful, sculpted face, that sable hair, those dark, long-lashed eyes and that skilled, sinful mouth…?

In two blissful, dreamlike weeks she had fallen so helplessly, so hopelessly in love that giving herself to Vito had been an act of homage, of adoration. She had clung to him, clasped his body to her, as his honeyed stroke had opened to her a heaven she had not even known existed, could ever exist.

And in the morning he had thrust her into hell.

A hell so agonising she had never known she could feel such pain.

She had awoken, naked in his arms, after he'd taken her through the gates of paradise itself, and lain dazed with bliss and happiness in the huge, ornate bed. Then, horror-struck, had heard the sound of the front door opening, and voices, felt Vito tensing suddenly, every muscle rigid, and then, like some slow, endless nightmare, the bedroom door had opened and her mother had walked in.

She could see, as if in slow motion, her mother's face frowning at the closed heavy drapes, her head turning to see the naked figures in the bed.

And recognition dawning on her horror-struck face.

Even now, seven years later, she could still feel the horror of it all. Still feel cold sweat break out down her spine.

Her mother screaming. Screaming with fury, with outrage. Enrico charging in, demanding to know what the hell was going on. Herself cowering, mortified, beneath the sheets covering her nakedness, wanting only to die.

And Vito.

Shameless. Unashamed.

Callous, uncaring.

So cruel.

She could hear him now. She would always hear him.

Her mother yelling at him in Italian, her face distorted. Enrico angry, his hand slashing through the air.

And Vito. Vito coolly climbing out of bed. Uncaring that he had not a stitch on. Pulling on his trousers and drawing up the zip with insolent unconcern.

Turning to Arlene.

'Seduce her?' he had drawled in a tight, hard voice, making sure he was speaking English so Rachel could understand it, understand *exactly* what he was saying. 'Hardly. She was gagging for it.'

Water splashed over her hands, jarring her back to the present. She shut her eyes, trying to block out the memory, block out the past.

But she couldn't. It was there now, piercing her flesh, those vile, ugly words searing through her again, as they had that hideous morning eight years ago. When she had finally, bitterly realised just what Vito Farneste had been doing all along.

Deliberately, cold-bloodedly taking her inexperienced, naïve, *gagging for it* eighteen-year-old self to bed for one purpose only.

To part her from her virginity.

And by so doing strike at the woman he loathed with every fibre of his being.

Her mother's words, hurled at her in that hideous after-math, when Vito and Enrico had gone, had stung like a whip.

'My God, you fool, Rachel. You *fool*!' Arlene had screamed at her. 'Couldn't you *see* what he was doing? Didn't you find it just a tiny, tiny bit suspicious that a man like Vito Farneste should show the *slightest* interest in an eighteen-year-old schoolgirl? Vito doesn't waste his precious time on anyone who isn't a supermodel or a film star! He's got women eating out of his hand! They queue up for the privilege! Couldn't you *see* he was that kind of man? Didn't you *realize* he couldn't *possibly* be interested in you?'

Her mother had shaken her daughter's shoulders, fingers digging into her skin.

'He got you into bed to get at *me*! He knows how protective I am of you! So he thought it would be really *amusing* to seduce you. He hates me like the plague—he'd do anything to get at me!'

Anything—even to the point of forcing himself to have sex with a schoolgirl virgin.

Who'd been gagging for it...

No!

By force of will she blocked her mind and switched on the kettle. She mustn't think, wouldn't think.

Not about the past seven years ago. Not about the past two hours ago.

How could I have gone to him and asked him to marry me? How could I have?

She must have been insane to think that she could force his hand like that.

Anguish buckled through her all the same.

But I had to try! I had to!

The force driving her to confront him this afternoon had been compelling. A force so great she had not been able to walk away from the obligation to at least make the attempt. Two emotions, each unbearable, twisted within her to make a formidable, unopposable imperative.

Grief.

And guilt.

Again, as she poured boiling water over the teabag slumped in the chipped mug, her hand shook and a wave of grief and pain washed over her.

Her mother was dying. Lying there in her hospital bed, her face and body ravaged by the rogue cells that were devastating her, consuming her. The cancer had spread so fast, and the chemotherapy and radiation treatment needed had been so aggressive that Rachel had not needed the drawn faces of the doctors to know that Arlene was losing the battle for life.

Vivid, ghastly in her mind's eye, sprang the image of her mother's ravaged face. Once so beautiful, so perfect, now gaunt with pain and disease.

And alongside the rawness of her grief came the bitterness of guilt.

In the years following that hideous debacle in Rome, when she was eighteen and Vito Farneste had coldly, callously used her as a weapon against his mother's hated rival, she had withdrawn almost completely from her mother.

Arlene had been vehement in her demand that Enrico force Vito to marry her—as though, Rachel thought, gall rising in her throat, she had been some kind of deflowered and disgraced Victorian maiden, 'ruined' for the rest of eternity without the saving sanctity of a wedding ring on her finger.

Of course Enrico had refused—refused to listen to his mistress's rantings—and Vito's scornful, mocking laughter had been even worse. Neither of them had given a toss, Rachel knew, that Arlene's bastard daughter had lost her virginity. And to Rachel her mother's ranting had been even more mortifying than Vito's treatment of her. Hadn't Arlene seen that?

But she'd been obsessed by her determination that Vito should marry the girl he'd seduced, however hopeless, however mortifying that determination had been to Rachel.

In the end she had bolted back to England—but not to school. She had gone to her aunt, whom her mother seldom contacted any more, finding her humble lifestyle grating, and got herself a job waiting tables in a Brighton café. From now on, she had vowed, she would be financially independent of Arlene—and that meant independent of Enrico Farneste.

And besides, she'd had one more impelling reason to sever links with Arlene...

Her mind sheered away from the memory. Too much grief on grief.

She had enough to keep her going now. And the guilt that went hand in hand with it.

Dully, she poked at the teabag with a teaspoon, watching the dark brown colour stain out through the hot water. She reached inside the tiny fridge, with its half-broken seal around the door, and extracted a carton of milk, pouring it into the mug and continuing stirring. Still running on automatic. Her mind a clouded turmoil of thoughts and feelings.

Guilt. Such a powerful, corrosive emotion. Eating like acid through her life. Accentuating and exacerbating her grief until the combination was unbearable—making her do the wildest, most insane things.

Like trying to force Vito Farneste to marry her.

Just to ease her mother's dying.

She lifted the teabag from the mug and dropped it into the sink, the teaspoon with it. Then, cradling the mug, she wandered back out into the centre of the room, crossing to the window. The net curtains veiled the back alley below, with its rubbish bins and flybown, flapping posters, scrumpled litter.

She had not felt guilty about cutting Arlene out of her life. Why should she have? She had swanned off with Enrico Farneste to live in elegant prostitution. With all the puritanical certainty of a teenager Rachel had known that there was no romance, nor remorse, to soften the brutal fact of Enrico's and Arlene's adultery—neither one of them had cared tuppence that Enrico still had a wife living, nor that Arlene was living her lavish existence as the kept mistress of another woman's rich husband.

She raised the mug to her mouth and sipped the hot tea, not even tasting it.

How wrong, how totally and completely wrong she had been about Arlene.

But she had not known that until too late.

Until her mother had become ill.

Then and only then had Rachel seen her mother in a quite different light.

'I did it all for you, my darling girl,' her mother had whispered, powerful painkillers making her mind wander and at the same time releasing, at last, the emotional detachment she had layered over herself all through Rachel's life.

'I wanted you to have something more than I ever had! Your father disowned you—despised me! Thought me some little council house tart, good enough for sex but nothing more! I hated him for that! Hated him! So I wanted you to grow up to be the kind of person he and his precious family could never despise! You were to have the best education, the best upbringing, mixing with the kind of people your father and his family were! And that's why I gave you his name—even though I couldn't put it down on the birth certificate. He knew I would never make a claim on him, or his precious estate. He disowned us both. When he smashed

himself up in that car of his I was glad! He'd had his pun-
ishment for what he'd done to you. To me. Refusing to be
your father. Laughing at me for not being good enough to
marry him!'

Arlene's hand clutched at Rachel's. Anguish seared in her
eyes.

'Why was I never good enough to marry? Why was I
only ever good enough for sex? Enrico never wanted me to
be anything other than his mistress! Never! I was good
enough for sex —that was all.'

The breath rasped in her throat, and her chest rose and
fell agitatedly. Rachel sat there, reeling, as her mother went
on to make her final, heart-rending confession.

'I loved Enrico so much! And he never loved me back.
Never! Not for a second, not a moment! I was just his mistress, that's all. I tried never to show I cared—if I showed
too much he got angry, annoyed. Thought I was trying to
pressure him to divorce his wife! But I knew he never
would. Not because she was a Catholic—or him!—but
because—' the bitterness was etched into her voice again
'—because even if he'd been free he would never have married me! I was just his mistress. Never good enough to
marry. Just good enough for sex.'

Rachel stood now, mug in hand, staring blindly. Anger
for her mother churned in her.

More memories pounded in her head. Her mother lying
there, eyes huge and strained in her gaunt, shrunken face,
her body so slight against the white of the sheets and pillow.
Her voice low and anguished as she'd spoken to her daughter, her hand clutching Rachel's.

'I wanted you to be good enough to marry. I wanted you
to be the kind of woman that men married, made their wife.
To be good for something more than sex. When Vito seduced you I nearly died... He'd taken you and used you,
tried to turn you into what Enrico had turned me into...'

Arlene's eyes closed, exhaustion and defeat in her face.

'I had a dream. So real I sometimes thought that it had actually happened. A dream that Vito would marry you— as his father would never marry me. I saw you as a bride— a Farneste bride! With the Farneste emeralds around your neck!'

Her mother's eyes flew open, feverish, over-bright.

'That's why I took them! They were there, in the Rome apartment—the apartment that Vito took you to, to try and make you someone like me—good enough for sex and nothing else! I was there when Enrico collapsed with his heart attack, and after the ambulance had taken him away I never saw him again. Never! Vito gave orders for me not to be allowed into the hospital. Not even to say goodbye. Not even to say that I loved him—though he had never wanted my love. Only my body. But Vito would not let me see him. He had me thrown out of the Rome apartment.

'I went back to the villa, and then, three days later, when I was eaten with fear for Enrico and what was happening to him—because when I phoned the hospital they would give me no news. Vito had ordered them not to! A black security van drove up to the villa. I was evicted. The day's newspaper had finally disclosed that Enrico Farneste of Farneste Industriale had died the day before in Rome, with his son and his ''beloved wife'' at his bedside! And I, his ''beloved mistress'', didn't even know. Didn't even know that Enrico had died. Until Vito had me thrown out of the villa, stripping me of everything that I'd had with Enrico.'

Arlene drew breath again, painful, rasping, and Rachel sat, holding her hand, her heart crushed in a vice, as she listened to her mother's unburdening.

'But Vito didn't know.' Arlene's eyes glittered again, fever-bright. 'Didn't know that I'd taken the emeralds with me to the villa, and when he threw me out I took them with me. They're yours, my darling girl! Yours! For when you are a Farneste bride.'

Rachel tried to protest, gently, carefully. But Arlene's morphine-clouded mind had created a new reality, one based entirely on final, desperate hope, however hopeless, however forlorn.

'It's my only wish for you,' she whispered, her eyes huge, flowing with maternal love so long held in check, repressed and suppressed. 'If I could see you as Vito's bride—oh, my darling girl—then I would die happy...'

Tears welled in Rachel's eyes as she stared blindly through the net curtains.

She might have been insane to think that she could force Vito Farneste to put a ring on her finger, even for so brief a time as what was left of Arlene's life, but for all that, for all her pathetic failure this afternoon, she knew with agonising certainty that she had been right to do what she had attempted. It might have been hopeless, ludicrous—as insane as Vito had so sneeringly dubbed it. But she would not have rested easily until and unless she had at least tried—*tried* to fulfil her mother's dying wish.

Death changes everything, she thought. It makes a new reality and destroys the old one. Gives new imperatives, new urgencies.

All that was important to her now was her mother's brief remaining span of time. Nothing else. Not herself. Not her feelings, or wishes, or fears.

Nor Vito Farneste's either.

They didn't count at all.

Nor did he.

The November night was bleak and dreary by the time Rachel returned from her visit to her mother. Every visit was painful, but today, after having endured the ordeal of trying to make her mother's hopeless dying wish come true, it had been even more so. Arlene had seemed weaker, and one of the nurses had let slip the word that Rachel had dreaded to hear.

Hospice.

Pain clutched her again as she walked into her shabby flat.

They had so little time left together—and they had wasted so much. Even now, knowing as she did why Arlene had packed her off to school, seen so little of her while she was growing up, it still hurt desperately.

'I didn't want you associated with me!' Arlene had told her, and Rachel's heart had been crushed with grief as she heard the truth about her mother's feelings for her. 'I didn't want you tainted by my relationship with Enrico! And—' her voice had darkened '—I didn't want that satyr Vito coming anywhere near you.'

Rachel cut the memory. It was too awful, too painful. Now, with the rawness of setting eyes on Vito again after so many years, the pain was exacerbated tenfold, scraping along her nerves. How right her mother had been to keep her away from Vito Farneste...

And yet even as her head spoke her heart betrayed her.

Vito—to see him again, a few hours ago, had been agony.

And ecstasy.

He had not changed—he would never change—he would always be to her what he had always been.

The most beautiful man in the world.

Through the consuming anguish of grief at her mother's illness another feeling thrust itself through.

This time around she knew what it was. When she'd been eighteen she hadn't even known its name, its existence. Now, at twenty-five, she did.

Desire.

Desire for a man who made her yearn to press against

him, to feel that lean, hard body against hers, to reach up and taste that beautiful, sinful mouth...

How can you want a man who despises you—who has always despised you? It's shameful, pathetic, unforgivable!

But knowing it and feeling it were two completely different things.

If only I hadn't gone today! If only I hadn't seen him again!

A sick longing went through her, shaming her.

She forced it aside. She would never set eyes on Vito Farneste again.

She had tried this afternoon to do what love for her mother had impelled her to do. It had been the most useless, mortifying experience, but at least she had tried! At least she would not have it on her conscience that she hadn't even summoned the courage to *try* and grant her mother's dying wish—impossible though she had always known it to be! She had failed—failed miserably—but at least it was over.

With a crushed, heavy heart she prepared her supper—baked beans and toast. Cheap, quick. When she had eaten, having had to force every mouthful, she fetched her laptop.

She'd never gone to the prestigious university she would no doubt have qualified for had she finished school. Instead she'd taken evening classes at a local college, funding them out of her waitress wages, until she'd had sufficient language qualifications to get a job in the marketing department of an international company. She had earned enough to put down a deposit on a tiny but comfortable flat in London. The same flat she had sold to help pay for her mother's private hospital treatment.

She gave a bitter smile. After the luxury that Enrico Farneste had kept her in, her mother's finances had not fared well. Perhaps grief, a broken heart and the bitterness that had consumed her mother had made her uncaring of the money she had put aside. Certainly it was running out fast

now—the expense of the private hospital was heavy—but
Rachel didn't care. Arlene would live in comfort for the rest
of her life...

She opened up the laptop and started to work. She had
found—and was grateful for it—freelance work, translating
marketing literature from Spanish and French. It wasn't well
paid, but it was flexible, and it allowed her to spend as much
time as she could with her mother. While she still could.

The out-of-tune sound of the battered Entryphone halted
her abruptly. Perturbed—for who on earth was wanting her
at this hour?—she went to the door and picked up the phone.

'Yes?' she answered guardedly. 'Who is it?'

'Vito Farneste,' came the terse reply.

CHAPTER FOUR

FOR about five frozen seconds Rachel just stood there, numb, unable to believe what she had just heard. Then she reached to press the button for entry to the front door of the house conversion downstairs. But even as she did so a shiver of fear went through her.

What did he want?

As she tentatively opened her bedsit door, two storeys up, she heard the rapid, decisive tread of his step on the uncarpeted staircase. A moment later he appeared around the corner of the stairs, heading straight up to her.

His face was dark and forbidding, and she felt even more nervous. Did he think she had the Farneste emeralds here, in the flat? Was he planning simply to help himself to them forcibly?

And anyway, how had he found out where she lived?

Agitation and turmoil made her blurt out the question aloud, even before he came up to her.

'How did you know where I lived?'

His mouth tightened as he approached her.

'I had you followed when you left. Is living here some kind of joke? Meant to deceive me?'

Vito walked up to her and all but pushed her aside to stride into the bedsit. His coruscating glance around its confined shabby space made his brows snap together.

His eyes swivelled to Rachel, standing stricken by the doorway.

Emotion churned in her like a washing machine gone mad, tumbling round and round inside her. Fear, shock, resentment, bewilderment—and something far more powerful

53

than any of those. A leaping of her blood that overpowered everything else going through her.

He was still wearing his business suit, but he'd discarded his tie since she had seen him that afternoon. Its lack made him look no less formidable, but somehow slightly raffish as well. So too did the graze of a shadow over his jaw. She felt her stomach clench.

He stood at the centre of the room, such as it was, given its narrow confines, his hands splayed at his waist, jacket pushed back.

'Why this dump? Are you really so broke? You didn't look it when you sailed into my office this afternoon. Or were you trying to impress me?'

There was a sneer in his voice.

Her face tightened. She was fighting hard for control, but she knew she was losing. Vito Farneste was the last person she'd expected to see here, and shock was making her stupid.

'Well?' he demanded, his eyes flickering over her.

This time there was disdain in them.

Rachel was not surprised. This afternoon she had looked as good as she knew she could. Now she was just about the opposite. She was wearing a grey track suit, her face was devoid of make-up, and her hair was drawn back into a tight, workmanlike, unflattering knot.

From somewhere she managed to find a retort to his demand.

'What business are my finances of yours?'

His eyes hardened. He was obviously not liking her tone of voice.

'Considering you just turned down a million euros from me, I would have thought your finances were indeed my concern. And, since you're not even going to get to first base with your ludicrous ''conditions'' you might as well take the money, no? Where are the emeralds?'

He looked around, his expression of disdain deepening—
as if, thought Rachel angrily, his precious family jewels
might be contaminated by being in such a lowly abode! But
then, she thought bitterly, he probably thought they'd been
contaminated already, just by having been in her mother's
possession.

'They're in a bank!' she answered sharply. 'Where else
do you think they'd be?'

'Which bank?'

She shook her head. 'I don't have to tell you that. If you
came here to try and get me to sell them to you, you can
get out! My mother will never sell!'

'Not even if it means you're so broke you're living in
this dump? Where is Arlene anyway? Is she broke too? I
can't imagine her letting her precious *bambina* live in this
place while she spends the rest of what she got from my
father!'

Rachel's face closed.

He mustn't find out about her mother. If he did, and
showed the slightest sign of satisfaction that his father's
hated mistress was reaping the wages of sin, she would kill
him with her bare hands...

An urgent, overwhelming need to protect her mother from
this man who hated her so much, when she was so pitifully
weak and vulnerable, consumed her.

'She's abroad!' she lied quickly. 'Spain. She likes warm
weather.'

She could feel Vito's gaze pressing on her.

'So how come you feel free to dispose of the emeralds?
Do you even have possession of them?'

'Yes,' answered Rachel baldly. She did have possession.
Arlene had granted her power of attorney over her affairs
two months ago, before her mother had become too ill to
look after them herself any longer.

So, yes, she had possession of the Farneste emeralds.

But she had known she could never sell them. Had known that when her mother was dead she would return them, gratis, to the one person to whom they truly belonged—Enrico's widow. She understood why her mother had taken them, but she knew that Arlene had no right to them, and nor did she.

Had Vito agreed this afternoon to her 'conditions' then she would have returned them in that fashion—she wanted nothing from Vito but his name on her wedding certificate, and wedding photos to show her mother, to convince her that she had truly married Enrico's son, that—however unlikely the notion was to anyone not at the extremity of life as Arlene was—she was going to be what Arlene had never been: a respected wife, not a mistress open to insults and sneers.

But Vito had shot down her ridiculous attempt to make her mother's dying wish come true. And so she must keep the emeralds until Arlene was dead, when she could return them to Signora Farneste.

As she answered him, something changed in his face—something that made her blood run colder.

'You do realise, don't you, that you have admitted that you are in possession of the Farneste emeralds, whose ownership by your mother I strongly dispute, whatever the total inadequacy of the law in that respect? So tell me, *cara mia*, what is to stop me *persuading* you to return them to me?'

There was a glitter in his eyes, and Rachel felt fear stab through her again. But she could not—must not—feel fear in front of him. Defiantly she shot back at him.

'I don't give squat what you think the law is about the emeralds! If you could have got them back legally by now you would have! And if you so much as lay a *finger* on me I'll have you done for assault so fast you won't have time to squeal! And the precious tabloids can go to town on the scandal!' She took a deep, shuddering breath. 'So if that's

all you came here for—to try out your bully-boy tactics—
you can clear out just as fast!'

The glitter in his eyes had intensified, and suddenly the
poky bedsit seemed even smaller than it was. Her breathing
had quickened, she could tell, and adrenalin was coursing
through her bloodstream.

It was because of the fear she was denying, the tension—
that was all.

But she knew she was deceiving herself. Adrenalin was
flowing in her veins for a quite different reason.

She could feel her body responding to his presence, feel
every nerve leap to quivering life.

It mortified her. She had to damp it down—hard. If Vito
saw it—saw her reacting to him—she would die, just die!
It would give him another weapon over her that she could
never hope to defeat.

Because she knew, with a terrible, sickening sense of
doom, that she would feel this way about Vito Farneste for
the rest of her life. She would never be able to stop the tide
of desire, of longing, of *wanting* pulsing through her whenever she was near him. She was in thrall to him, and it was
a captivity she could never escape.

Like a magnet, the dark glitter in his eyes drew her—and
frightened her.

But his next words frightened her even more.

And sent a humiliating, debilitating shiver down her
spine.

'I was thinking,' he said, and his voice, out of nowhere,
was a dark purr, 'of a quite different method of persuasion,
cara mia.'

His dark eyes rested on her, and in them she saw an
expression that ripped the years away. Her stomach hollowed out, her legs going instantly shaky.

Desperately she struggled against its bone-dissolving
effect.

It was fake then and it's fake now! Fake, fake, fake!

He put it on then, when you were eighteen, fooling you that he found an eighteen-year-old English schoolgirl virgin attractive, and he's putting it on now!

Besides, she knew what she looked like right now—the glossy finery she had worn this afternoon had gone, and she was back to the way nature had made her, with a passion-killer track suit and her hair pulled back into a stark knot, and not a scrap of make-up to soften the image.

He saw her reaction and it amused him, she could see, but beneath the humour anger was running—she could sense that too.

She watched him walk towards her. There was purpose in his stride, and she felt again that rush of adrenalin that so shamed her. She wanted to move, jerk away, scream, shout, run out of the door, back away to the end of the bed, lock herself in the tiny bathroom—anything to get away from him.

But she was rooted to the spot, and as she stood there he stopped in front of her. The glitter in his eyes quickened her breathing.

Even as he halted his hand reached out, curving around the nape of her neck, and to her shame, her everlasting, shuddering shame, she felt her head bow slightly, as if to ease the cool, exquisite sliding of his fingers along the sensitive skin at the back of her neck.

Sensation dissolved through her in a drowning rain, washing away every long, long year of the seven that had passed since Vito Farneste had last caressed her.

Her eyes drooped closed. She was unable to resist the temptation of the silken, sensuous glide of his fingers, the delicate stroking of their tips against her quivering skin.

She heard him murmur something in Italian. She did not know what it was. Her entire battery of senses were coalesced into a single sense—touch.

His other hand curved around her jaw and cheek, lifting her face. Helplessly her eyes fluttered open again, and she watched, caught in that silken, sensuous thrall, as he lowered his head.

His mouth moved on hers like velvet—softest, smoothest velvet—and the drowning rain dissolved through her, taking her into a realm where she had never thought to walk again.

It was bliss, it was paradise, it was a heaven so exquisite she could not think, could not move, could only…succumb. Succumb to the wordless, timeless bliss of being kissed by Vito Farneste. She felt her body lose all its strength, and start to sink forward against his. Surrendering to everything, everything that was Vito, that was his beauty, his thrall and his temptation.

His kiss deepened, his tongue gliding inside her mouth, shooting through her such strong sensations that she felt she must swoon like some Victorian maiden overcome by something far beyond her experience.

But she was no Victorian maiden. No maiden at all—thanks to Vito Farneste. Thanks to the man who was standing here, one hand curved around her neck, the other holding her mouth up to him, while he took his pleasure in her…

Except that it would not be pleasure to him.

No answering bliss would be dissolving his nerves. No sensuous helplessness would be holding him motionless while he gave himself to this endless, exquisite sensation…

For him this would be something quite, quite different.

It means nothing to him—nothing at all! He's just doing it for the same reason he did it the last time—to make use of me.

Last time he wanted to use me to wound my mother.

This time he wants the Farneste emeralds…

With a strength she did not know how she'd found, Rachel pulled sharply away.

'No!'

She pushed his arms from her, stepping backwards. Her heart was racing, her limbs shaking, and she had to fight for control.

For a second something moved in Vito's eyes, then it was gone. In its place was a familiar look—a mocking look.

'No? Well, that's a new word for you, *cara mia*. It was always, "Please, Vito—please!" All through the night!'

A smile twisted at his mouth—as mocking as the expression in his eyes.

She whitened.

This time it was not sexual humiliation that scalded in her memory—the vile humiliation of being told that she'd been 'gagging for it'.

This memory was worse.

So much worse.

She remembered, with vivid, hideous clarity, the last time she had said those words to Vito.

It hadn't been the time he was thinking of now, when she'd begged him for his touch, his caress.

It had been a quite, quite different occasion.

She had spoken the words over the phone, the impersonal, distancing phone, which was all that he had permitted. She had pleaded with his secretary to put her through, and maybe something in her abject distress and despair had softened the woman's well-trained heart, for she had indeed put her through. She hadn't announced her, knowing full well, Rachel had realised, that Vito would not want the call. So he had picked up his phone not knowing she was on the other end.

She heard again his curt, accented voice saying, 'Who is this?'

Her own trembling voice saying, 'It's Rachel—please, Vito—please—'

He had hung up. Not letting her say another word.

Let alone what she had steeled herself so desperately to tell him.

He had never let her get through to him again. From then on his secretary had been unswervingly adamant—Signor Farneste would take no calls from her.

As for Rachel's letter to him—a last, pitiful resort to get in touch with him—it had been returned to her inside another envelope, unopened, with a typed notice from his secretary saying that Signor Farneste would not accept any future attempt at communication from her, by whatever means.

And Rachel, in that moment, had accepted that to Vito she had ceased to exist.

Now, seven years later, he stood in front of her again.

Taunting her.

Her face shuttered, blocking out every emotion she felt about him, keeping them locked inside her, where they could do the least damage. She did not need them when it came to Vito Farneste and what she wanted from him—or what he wanted from her.

'Well, I'm saying no now, Vito,' she answered, her throat tight. 'I'm afraid the Farneste emeralds are worth a bit more than a quick tumble with the fabulous Vito Farneste. You're not getting them back that cheaply!'

His face hardened, the mocking look intensifying.

'The emeralds may be worth more—but you are not.'

It was one blow too many—but nothing in comparison with the other verbal blows he had struck her with in the past.

She did not flinch this time.

'Tough,' she said. Her voice was hard. It had to be. She took a sharp intake of breath. 'So, if that was your best offer, it's no sale. Along with the million euros.'

His attention was riveted at that.

'Why?' he shot at her. 'You live in a dump. A million euros would get you out of here—and then some!'

He was looking at her, narrow-eyed, intent. Trying to read her. Danger fluttered around her. Not the danger she had faced—faced down—a moment ago. A different danger.

A surge of protectiveness went through her, for her vulnerable, dying mother. He wanted to understand why she demanded such a ludicrous price for returning the emeralds.

He must never know.

She wouldn't expose her mother—even remotely—to this man.

Instinctively she led him away from the truth of why she had uttered such an outrageous demand. Marriage in exchange for the Farneste emeralds.

'So would marrying you. Get me out of here.'

Her voice was flat, her eyes holding his. Willing him to take that as her reason.

She watched his expression change, taking on that mocking, derisive look.

'So that is your ambition, is it?' His voice was a drawl. 'Being a mistress, like your mother, isn't enough for you. You want respectability…'

It was so close to the truth that he could see it in her eyes, she knew. Her chin lifted.

'Why not? As Signora Farneste I would be received everywhere.'

She didn't know why she'd said that, continuing with this farce. Vito Farneste would no more marry her than fly her on wings to the moon.

His laugh was derisive.

'Oh, ambitious indeed! And tell me, Little Miss Golddigger, do your ambitions extend to getting your share of the Farneste money, courtesy of a lavish divorce settlement?'

She didn't let that jibe hit her either.

'No,' she said in the same flat voice.

'No? So you would be prepared to marry me even if I threw you out after six months without a penny in alimony?'

His disbelief was evident.

'Yes,' she answered doggedly.

'Why, *cara mia*, how flattered I should be—you prefer me to a million euros hard cash, and you want me so much you'll even forgo your alimony!'

His mockery snapped something in her—something she'd been holding on to tightly.

Never, *never* again would she let him mock her stupid, helpless, gullible desire for him!

'This isn't about *you*, Vito! I don't give a damn about *you*!'

His eyes darkened.

Recklessly she went on, unable to stop herself, unwilling to bear the thought that Vito Farneste thought she was so desperate for him she was prepared to use the Farneste emeralds to get him.

'There's someone far more important to me than you! Someone—'

She stopped dead, appalled at what she had nearly burst out with.

For a second there was total silence, and then, in a voice that made her flesh shrivel, Vito spoke.

'Finally I see what game you're trying to play. This sudden craving for respectability.'

Hurriedly, desperately, she tried to claw back what she had so stupidly blurted out.

'No—I—'

A hand slashed through the air.

'Too late, *cara mia*. I can see now what you're up to. This isn't about marrying *me*—it's about marrying someone else. Or rather him refusing to marry you. Your lover refuses to marry you—a prudent man, given your background!—so you think you can get your own back on him by suddenly becoming Signora Farneste! You don't want a million euros, and you don't want alimony—you want revenge! How does the saying go? *Hell hath no fury like a woman scorned.* That's what this is all about. You getting your own back on a man who's scorned you. Who wants you as a mistress—not a wife.'

She stared, trying to take in what he was saying. Adding two and two and coming up with a number so bizarre she could not at first work out what he was saying.

Vito was still speaking.

'Finally I get the picture. Now it makes sense. For such a prize—revenge: the sweetest dish of all!—you were willing to come sliming into my office today! Thinking that dangling my emeralds in front of me would lure me to the altar!'

The scorn dripped from him like acid. His eyes flicked over her contemptuously.

'You were really going to do a number on him, weren't you? Make him think you'd found a rich man willing to marry you—*and* enjoy you in bed, too! And to get me to go along with this delightful scheme you offered me back my own emeralds and the dubious pleasures of your body.'

His contempt stung her into words. From somewhere—she did not know where—she found a scorn to equal his own. Her head tilted slightly, and she eyed him tauntingly.

'Actually, no. It was only the emeralds you were going to get, Vito.' Biting indifference infused her voice. 'Sex with you wasn't going to be part of the deal. Once was enough, you know? Been there, done that, got the Vito Farneste T-shirt. I don't want another one. I've moved on.'

She knew she hadn't the weapons to fight him with. Only this one. All she had. It was frail, and it was pathetic, but it was all she could do. Feign indifference to him. God alone knew where he'd come up with the idea that she wanted to marry him in order to punish some mythical lover who wouldn't marry her. But she wasn't going to refute it. It would serve to protect the truth about her real reason.

And the lie about her indifference to him would protect her further.

Since this entire conversation was pointless, and all she desperately wanted was for Vito Farneste to walk out of her life again, as he had walked out once before—with no looking back, none, not once—it didn't matter what she said. So long as it got rid of him.

And left her with something—anything—the barest shreds of her pride.

Like a beggar searching for scraps, she took refuge in another insult.

'I know you think you're God's monumental gift to women, Vito, but I'm afraid as far as I'm concerned you're a bit of a yawn. I only wanted your ring on my finger, that's all. Not your stud services—magnificent as you consider them.'

He was looking at her. Eyes resting on her. Expressionless. His face expressionless.

She shifted uneasily. What was happening? Why was he looking at her like that? Without any expression in his face at all?

She'd expected a flash of anger, something that would show her just how much he objected to having his sexual irresistibility insulted.

But he was just looking at her, his face completely closed. Uneasiness snaked through her again. Then she realised what he was doing—he was deliberately not responding to her feeble little jibe just to show her how trivial it was. What did Vito Farneste care about what Rachel Vaile thought of his prowess in the bedroom? Her opinion was of no value. It never had been.

And it certainly wasn't now. She was like some pathetic little gnat, buzzing at him.

A dart of anger went through her. She was of little account to Vito—had always been of little account—nothing but his father's whore's bastard daughter...

She provoked him again. Something compelled her to get a reaction from him—any reaction! To show that she could have *some* effect on him, even if it were only a hundredth of a hundredth of the kind of effect he could have on her just by glancing at her with those dark, devastating eyes.

'I suppose you think I was besotted with you when I was eighteen, don't you?' She gave a light laugh. God knows how she dug it out of herself, but she did all the same. 'Well—' she gave a little shrug '—this time around you can see I'm not besotted! The big Latin Lover act is wasted on me. Oh,' she conceded, knowing she had to outface him all the way down the line or shrivel to ashes, 'I was curious just now, letting you kiss me, but as for anything more... I don't think so. And now, if you don't mind, I have things to get on with.'

She walked to the door, feeling amazed, disbelieving, that her legs were still working. She had to get him out of here—she was desperate for that. She just wanted him gone. So she could collapse alone. In private. In safety.

She pulled back the automatic lock on the door and yanked it open, standing aside.

Then she looked back at Vito.

He hadn't moved.

He was just standing there with that same expressionless face. A silent shiver went through her. How had she *dared* say such things to him as she just had? Where had such lies come from? And what use had they been anyway? she thought bitterly. She could have stabbed a carving knife in him and he wouldn't have reacted to her! A few stupid, sarcastic insults from her weren't even worth him getting angry over.

'Do you think you could shift yourself?' she prompted.

She stared at him, not understanding why he wasn't moving.

His face was closed. Quite blank. His body seemed very still. Then, abruptly, he started to stroll towards the door. She felt herself tense as she readied herself for him walking past her, so close. But when he was a metre or so from her he halted, reached out a hand, and casually pushed the door she was holding shut.

'What—?'

Her start of consternation was cut off. Vito spoke right across her. His blank, unreadable eyes rested on her quite expressionlessly. His voice was a drawl

'You had better contact your bank tomorrow and instruct them to release the emeralds. Phone my PA with the bank's location so she'll know where to send the courier.'

Rachel stared disbelievingly.

'I have no intention,' she bit out, 'of letting you have the emeralds!'

He raised an eyebrow.

'Every Farneste bride wears the emeralds on her wedding day. Do you imagine I'm going to let you be an exception?'

There was mockery in his eyes, cold, hard mockery, as they rested on her.

Her mouth opened, then closed, her throat moving. Her brain seemed to have stopped working. Her heart had stopped beating.

'It will be a civil wedding, as soon as the law permits, and will be dissolved again as soon as legally feasible. Oh, there'll be a pre-nup you'll have to sign, and the emeralds must be around your neck when I marry you so that you can return them to me afterwards.' He reached for the door and drew it open again.

He smiled into her shock-frozen face—a smile completely devoid of pleasure.

'You should be looking happy, *cara mia*—your girlish dreams have just come true… I'm going to marry you.'

He strolled past her, out of the flat, down the stairs. He looked relaxed, stepping with lithe grace down the shabbily carpeted staircase, his Latin elegance totally out of place in the run-down house.

Numbly Rachel watched him let himself out of the front door, heard it thud shut behind him.

After a long, long while she felt her heart start to beat again.

CHAPTER FIVE

VITO eased himself into the back seat of the car, and his driver pulled away from the kerb.

Anger iced through him.

So, Rachel Vaile—alias Rachel *Graham*!—thought she could use him as a patsy. Twist him to her purposes the way her cursed mother had twisted his father! Right up to the moment of his death.

A hard, vicious knot tugged deep inside him. Arlene Graham had killed his father as sure as if she'd held a gun to his head. His fatal heart attack had been triggered, so the cardiac specialist at the hospital had informed him, avoiding eye contact, by the strain of strenuous coitus.

Or, to put it in the vernacular, over-active sex with his mistress.

The paparazzi and the Italian gutter press had had a field-day! Gloating over every last tasty morsel of a high-life scandal that combined sex, wealth, adultery and death all in one rich package. His mother's humiliation had been complete.

He had got what satisfaction he could from having Arlene ejected from the Rome apartment and then from the villa.

And in revenge she'd taken the emeralds.

The anger iced through him again

Well, he was getting them back now—but that was not why he was marrying Rachel Vaile. She could have rotted in hell before she'd manipulate him like that!

His brow darkened.

No, getting the emeralds back was just a bonus.

The real meat was a quite different dish.

And, like revenge, best eaten cold.

Rachel Vaile. Delectable. Desirable.

And very, very beddable.

A slow, hard smile slid across his mouth. She really shouldn't have tried to challenge him like that, telling him she wasn't interested in him sexually. Not when he had been able to see her whole body vibrating with a sensual pulse that had made his own body surge, even before she had dissolved into that kiss.

He was going to take great pleasure in demonstrating to her, quite consummately, how totally wrong she was...

That was why he was going to indulge her by marrying her.

To taste one more time the honey that she promised.

And when he had tasted it to the full he would do what he had done last time around.

Let her rot in hell.

He owed her that much, at least.

Rachel stared out of the porthole. Fluffy white clouds made the scene look like something out of a children's cartoon. A bright white sun blazed down over the cloudscape, dazzling her eyes.

She wondered what she was feeling, and decided in the end that she wasn't feeling anything—except a numbed stunnedness that she was actually sitting here, on a privately hired executive jet, winging towards the Caribbean.

And her marriage to Vito Farneste.

She should be feeling triumphant. Grovellingly relieved. Disbelieving that she had actually succeeded in getting him to accede to her crazy, absurd plan.

But all she could feel was anaesthetised.

She shifted slightly in the wide leather seat. Apart from the hum of the engines it was very quiet in the cabin. Across the aisle Vito was sitting, ignoring her totally, working through a stack of papers on the table in front of him.

He'd said hardly anything to her since she'd been deposited at Northolt airfield earlier that morning by the car he'd sent for her, and his expression was unreadable. Well, she thought sourly, what *did* you say to a woman you loathed, a woman you'd deliberately seduced to wound her mother, with whom you were now going through a travesty of a wedding service simply to get back a family heirloom? Normal conversation wasn't exactly on the cards, was it?

Memory tugged at her, though she tried to stop it. Memories of Vito, in Rome, a lifetime ago, in that dreamtime that surely had never really happened... When she'd been at such magical ease in his company, laughing and talking and never, never running out of conversation...as if he took real pleasure in her company...

Fake—it had all been fake. He'd been stringing her along, silly little English schoolgirl, that was all.

She eased her ankles, rotating one and then the other. The movement shifted the heavy document lying on her lap. Vito had handed it to her as she'd taken her seat.

'The pre-nup,' he'd said laconically, his eyes dark and inexpressive. 'No wedding without your signature on it.'

She'd read it through. It contained no surprises. The Farneste emeralds would become the unconditional property of Vito Farneste the moment the ceremony was complete. And when the marriage ended she would take nothing with her—not a cent. She had no claim whatsoever on the Farneste fortune, and undertook never to use the Farneste name, or to speak to any member of the press about her marriage or the Farneste family.

She would sign it without a second thought.

And then she would marry him.

She was still stunned at how swiftly he'd moved. They were going to Antillia, a small island state in the Caribbean, he'd informed her tersely. It had two main advantages. Couples could get married instantly, without the wait that UK law stipulated, and—again unlike in the UK—pre-nuptial contracts were watertight under Antillian law.

The numbness closed over her again, the sense of dulling unreality.

I can't think about this, she thought. I can't and I mustn't. It's too unreal, too bizarre, too...

Too painful.

The words sounded in her mind, and she could not stop them.

In your dreams...

The haunting phrase echoed round her head. She felt her heart clutch.

She was going to marry a man who had once, for a brief, illusory spell, been all the world to her! A man she had given her first love to.

A man who had deliberately, calculatingly, betrayed that love, mocked and destroyed it.

And now she was going to go through—deliberately, calculatingly—with a wedding ceremony that would mock her for the rest of her life.

But it's not for me! It's for my mother! I have to do this. I have to! It's absurd, it's horrible, it's ludicrous. But it's all I can do. I can't refuse to do it!

Heaviness closed over her like a dull weight, pressing down on her.

She has so little time left— I have to do whatever I can, whatever it is, to make her happier. It doesn't matter about me—it only matters about her...

Grief stabbed at her, buckling her face.

She went on staring out at the clouds.

Something made Vito look up from his work. He'd buried himself in some highly complex proposals for a joint venture with a Far Eastern manufacturer the moment he'd boarded the plane. Anything to take his mind off what he was doing.

Unreality kept washing through him. He must be mad to do what he was doing! He should simply call the stewardess and give orders for the plane to turn around and head back to London. Then dump Rachel Vaile on the tarmac and walk away. For ever.

But he didn't. Instead he went on leafing through the proposals, making notes, jotting down queries, questions that needed answers, points for his lawyers. A grim smile played over his mouth. Running Farneste Industriale was no sinecure. It was hard, relentless work, with a crushing responsibility for his workforce, whose livelihoods depended on him, and the company contributed to a significant tranche of the Italian economy.

No wonder my father needed his R&R! Escape times with a beautiful woman to take his mind off work...

The thought came to him unwillingly, but with that same humourless smile he acknowledged the truth of it. The devil was that it hadn't been his wife that his father had turned to for such R&R.

No, don't go down that path. He'd walked it barefoot, over every thorn, for too many years. His mother's heartbreak, his father's defection. And he'd been powerless to do anything about it. Anything except accuse and despise.

And offer what comfort he could to his mother.

She'd suffered in silence. Only those debilitating attacks that had come, far too coincidentally, with his father's sojourns with his mistress had shown him her distress. When they'd come she had retired from the palatial Farneste residence outside Turin to the family's chalet in the Italian Alps, high above Lake Como, to pine for her faithless husband in silent, lonely misery. She hadn't even wanted her son with her to keep a vigil.

While Arlene Graham had lived the gilded life of a golden whore on his father's wealth…

And now he was about to marry her daughter.

Emotion scythed through him. Bitter with gall.

He lifted his head from his work and turned to look at her.

Her face was averted.

And the expression on it stilled him completely.

She should have been radiating triumph, believing she had brought him to heel with the promise of returning his own property to him. She should have been sitting there like a cat in possession of a rich bowl of cream, purring in anticipation of her victory.

But her face was etched like stone, every feature drawn, her gaze seeing something not physically visible through the porthole.

Something churned inside him. Clawed at him.

Something trying to be let out.

He twisted his head away sharply.

Rachel Vaile had no power over him! No power over his emotions.

Only his senses.

He sat back, deliberately relaxing his limbs. Closing his eyes.

Conjuring up her image, even though she was only a few feet away from him.

With deliberate studiedness he drew her image in his mind, delineating her graceful, sensuous body, skimming in his mind over the soft swell of her breasts, the rounded curve of her hip.

In the years since he had last laid eyes on her she had ripened—ripened like a peach to perfection. And tonight, oh, yes, tonight, under the Caribbean moon, he would taste her succulence.

And she would discover why he had agreed to marry her.

*   *   *

Rachel was dreaming. The long hours in the plane had finally lulled her to sleep. In her dream it was warm—beautifully warm. She was wearing a yellow sundress, short and flirty, leant to her by Zara, with narrow spaghetti straps. She was running up the Spanish Steps, nimbly avoiding the hordes of tourists sitting there simply because they were such a famous Roman landmark. Brilliant red flowers tumbled out of pots that lined the edge of the steps. A man stopped in front of her, holding out a single rose to sell, but she just smiled and darted round him. Behind her she could hear Vito catching up with her, despite the head start he had given her.

By the time she got to the top he had overtaken her, striding up on his long, powerful legs. He caught her arms as she stepped onto the final level terrace at the head of the long flight.

'You win!' She laughed. 'So I'll buy the next *gelato*!'

Warm, dark eyes had smiled down at her.

Smiling, smiling…

She felt her heart squeeze with happiness, catch with joy.

Vito… Vito…

She breathed his name silently, like a paean of praise. Praise for being Vito, the most gorgeous, beautiful, fantastic man in the world.

Who was choosing her, *her*, to spend his days with.

And the most magical night of her life with…

The scene shifted.

She was in his arms and he was making love to her. Making love so exquisitely her body was bathed in fire, aching with longing, flooded with yearning. He stroked her body, murmuring to her in words she did not understand but which sang like a song in her heart.

She felt herself blossom like a flower.

Then Vito was gone. Someone was shaking her shoulder, gently but insistently.

She opened her eyes, blinking, confused.

'I'm very sorry to have to wake you, madam,' a polite voice was saying, 'but we've started our descent and you will need to fasten your seat-belt.'

Reality came sweeping back to her as she saw the flight attendant straighten. Beyond her, Vito was still working at his papers, as though he had done nothing but that all the voyage. She felt her heart catch, her mind still full of the dream she had been woken from. For a moment she just gazed, as adoring of him now as she had been at eighteen, worshipping his cool, dark beauty.

She wanted to reach out her hand, touch him. Hold him. But she could not. Never again.

He was only a few feet away from her, but he might have been a thousand miles distant.

A terrible sadness went through her. Then bitterness came, lacing poisonously.

Don't get sentimental! He was never the man you thought he was. Never! Everything you thought you'd shared was fake. He was taking you for a fool every moment he was with you. Until the final moment. When he revealed his true self. That was the real Vito Farneste. And it still is.

That was what she had to remember.

All she had to remember. She forced herself to recall what she had told herself when she had gone to him in his executive office.

This is a business transaction, nothing more. No emotions are necessary.

She wondered why she had to keep repeating it to herself.

The plane started to bank steeply as it approached the runway, heading for their destination. Rachel could see a blue-green expanse of sea, and sunlight dazzling as the plane levelled again, dipping down more sharply into the last descent. Then, out of nowhere it seemed, land suddenly appeared, palm trees and greenery, miniature at first, but rapidly becoming full-sized as the plane glided down to earth.

They landed with only the slightest of bumps, and then the engine thrust went into reverse, braking them. She sat back, waiting till it was all over.

As she emerged from the plane, stepping down the shallow staircase, heat enveloped her. A balmy, subtropical heat, bringing with it a mix of scents—aircraft fuel and something exotically floral.

The heat and beauty seemed to mock her, utterly out of keeping with what she was about to do.

Immigration was swift at the small and almost deserted airport, and within minutes they were inside an air-conditioned car, their meagre luggage installed in the boot. Idly, Rachel wondered where they were going, and then realised it did not matter. She sat back in her corner of the seat, as physically far away from Vito as she could.

He did not speak to her, and she was glad.

They had nothing to say to each other.

In her handbag, nestled in a velvet bag, secure within a zippered compartment, lay the Farneste emeralds. The sole reason she was here, in the Caribbean, with a man she hated more than any man on earth.

A man she would marry this evening.

Rachel still felt too dazed and depressed to take in more than palm trees, the bumpy tarmac road and fields of what she assumed was sugar cane at either side. Then, a few minutes later, a flash of brilliant blue-green assailed her eyes and the car drew up at the edge of a quay by the ocean. A few rather ramshackle buildings clustered around the quay. Tied up there was an open motorboat.

Rachel frowned. What on earth—?

'We're going on to Ste Pierre—it's an offshore island which specialises in wedding parties.' Vito's inexpressive voice provided an unasked-for explanation.

She said nothing. There was nothing to say. Instead she got out of the car and into the boat. She sat down on the padded seat that curved around the gunwale and deliberately closed her eyes, lifting her face to the sun. The sea breeze cooled her face, and she felt the boat dip as Vito and the driver climbed down after her. There was some movement as the luggage was loaded, then the car driver was transformed into a boat driver and they set off. Vito, she was glad to note through cautiously half-opened eyes, was sitting well away from her.

The journey wasn't long—possibly fifteen minutes or so, Rachel estimated—and then the boat was pulling up at another quay. This time as she emerged she saw that the landing at Ste Pierre was much more picturesque—and so was the transport that awaited them. A pony and trap, with an awning over bright yellow seats, and a coachman in a wide-brimmed matching hat and open-necked shirt which contrasted vividly with his dark skin.

'Welcome to Ste Pierre—or Honeymoon Island to you folks!' the coachman announced with a beaming smile, in a strong Caribbean accent.

Feeling both an idiot and a hypocrite, Rachel let the boatman help her up into the trap, making sure she sat as near the far edge of the seat as possible.

This journey was even shorter, a bare five minutes, and all it did was convey them around the headland into the next bay. But as they came past the screening palm trees Rachel could not prevent an exclamation of pleasure breaking out.

The bay was beautiful! Like something out of a tourist brochure. The sea was turquoise here, vivid and bright, and lapped onto a beach that was dazzling in its whiteness. Set back from the beach, framed by palm trees and fronted by

scarlet flowers and lush greenery, was a low white planta-
tion-style building.

Their driver turned and beamed.

'Honeymoon House, folks!' he announced.

For a hotel, Rachel thought, it was on the small side. But
maybe they aimed at exclusivity rather than numbers. It certainly looked deserted, she realised, and there was no one
in the large oval-shaped pool just behind the beach in front
of the lawn. The horse—which had its own yellow straw
sunhat, slit to allow its long ears to poke through—went
clopping steadily along the narrow, unmetalled roadway. It
did not pass in front of the hotel, but headed inland to go
around to the rear of the building. Here, a carriage sweep
led to large white double doors shaded by a columned por-
tico, beneath which the coachman halted the vehicle.

The doors opened wide and a very upright Antillian
emerged, looking for all the world, Rachel registered, like
a Victorian butler. He came up to the trap, poised to help
the arrivals down. Vito sprang down lithely on his own, but
Rachel was glad of the butler's pristinely white-gloved
hand.

'Welcome to Honeymoon House, sir, madam,' he announced in a stately voice. 'Permit me to show you to your
rooms.'

Rachel caught the use of the plural word and felt a shiver
of relief go through her. She hadn't known what to expect,
but Vito had obviously stipulated separate rooms, however
strange that might be to a hotel that specialised in instant
Caribbean weddings.

As they went indoors Rachel looked around at the spa-
cious hallway, with its dark mahogany wood and white-
painted high ceiling. It was cooler here, yet it was not the
chill of air-conditioning. She felt a breeze blow through the
large airy room.

She frowned slightly. The hotel was beautifully furnished

and appointed, and was clearly an expensive place to stay—
but then Vito was a rich man; no need for him to go slum-
ming just because he was marrying a woman like her! But
it looked completely deserted. There was no sign of a reception desk, let alone other guests or even staff.

She followed the butler, who announced in the same
stately tones that his name was André and that he was entirely at their service during their stay, then led the way
down a wide corridor to the right and paused outside a door.

'Madam's room,' he intoned, and opened the door to
usher her in.

She went in gratefully, and could not help looking around
with pleasure. White louvred wardrobes lined one wall, an
electric fan flicked lazily in the centre of the high ceiling,
and a large, graceful four-poster bed stood swathed in voile.
André advanced, throwing open the white window shutters.

The vista beyond was beautiful. A white-painted veranda
edged the room, and beyond it a path led directly to the
paved pool area, where the water sparkled in the sunshine.
In the near distance, the turquoise sea dazzled her eyes.

It was a world away from London, in its winter bleakness,
and for some quite unaccountable reason Rachel felt her
spirits lift.

André murmured something. She smiled abstractedly and
stepped out onto the veranda to get a better look at the view.
When, after a few moments, she turned, she found she had
the room to herself. Her small suitcase stood on the rack.

Instinct took over. She hurried across to the case and
threw it open. Once she'd learnt that she was going to have
to go through with this travesty of a wedding not in a
London register office but on an instant wedding island in
the Caribbean, she had included her swimsuit in her luggage. Swimming would help to pass the time—and keep her
away from Vito.

She rummaged roughly through the suitcase's contents

and pulled out her costume. Five minutes later she was heading out to the swimming pool.

Gliding into the water was bliss. She let her hair stream in the water, the air cooling her wet face. Despite the warmth, no other hotel guests came out to share the pool with her. Relaxing in the balmy liquid, she turned over onto her back and floated, feeling some of the knotted tension at the ordeal she knew she must face that evening ease out of her. After a while she felt the weightless drift of her body bump her gently against the edge of the pool. Lazily she turned and rested her forearms on the tiled surround, pushing her streaming hair from her face. She blinked the water from her eyes and lifted her head slightly to gaze back across the greenery to the hotel.

And there, walking along the path towards her, was Vito.

Time contracted, dissolved.

Eleven years became an eye-blink.

She was fourteen years old again, and the most beautiful man in the world was walking towards her.

There was a roaring in her head, and for a brief, extraordinary moment she really did think that she had slipped back in time, had become again that teenage girl, gazing dumbstruck at the Italian male approaching her with lithe, careless grace.

Just like before he was wearing dark glasses, and as before his chinos were superbly cut, his pale shirt turned up at the cuffs, exposing lean wrists, and open at the neck. Only the sweater draped around his shoulders was missing.

As she gazed, frozen, as dumbstruck now as she had been then, he paused, his veiled eyes suddenly shifting from the sea beyond to where she clung at the side of the pool.

And then he too seemed to freeze.

Was he remembering? Rachel found herself thinking wildly. Remembering that moment eleven years ago?

Or was he simply repulsed by seeing her now, when he

might have thought her having a shower or resting on her bed?

She didn't wait to decide, simply let herself drop back into the water, feet touching the bottom of the pool as she twisted lengthwise and started to swim with jerky movements towards the seaward end of the pool. Doggedly she went on, swimming up and down, losing count. When she finally allowed herself to stop there was no sign of Vito.

The sun was visibly lower too. It was still warm, but the sea breeze ruffled over her wet skin as she emerged from the pool and she gave a little shiver. The shadows were lengthening and the sun was becoming more golden. She wrapped her towel around her, picked up her bag, feeling by its weight that the necklace was still safely within, and headed back to her room.

She had just showered and washed her hair when she heard a rap on the door from inside the bathroom.

She opened it cautiously, having wrapped her hair in a turban and wound a bath sheet concealingly around her.

Vito stood in the bedroom, obviously waiting for her to emerge.

She tensed instantly.

His dark glasses were gone, but his eyes, when they rested on her, were as veiled as if he had still been wearing them.

'Yes?' she said stonily.

He went on looking at her for a moment, and she started to feel even more uncomfortable. He could see nothing of her except her shoulders and bare arms, yet it was too much.

A sense of panic suddenly swept through her. What on earth was she doing here, four or five thousand miles from London, about to marry a man who loathed her as much as she loathed him? She couldn't go through with it! She couldn't! It didn't matter how brief the marriage was to be, how totally fake, she just couldn't do it!

Anyone, *anyone* else she could marry—but not Vito Farneste. Please, no. Not Vito…

He hurt me so much—I can't take the pain! I just can't!

She could feel it eating through her like acid, burning through the years, burning her skin, her flesh. Her heart.

Her mouth began to tremble.

'The wedding ceremony takes place in an hour and a half. Make sure you are ready.'

His words cut through the sudden debilitating weakness that had, out of nowhere, swept over her. She bit down on her lip, translating mental pain into physical, forcing herself back to that state of preternatural, emotionless calm that she knew it was essential she hang on to while she was here.

There was something wrong with his voice, she registered. It was as harsh as it always was when he spoke to her, but it was not that that made it different. She didn't know what it was—could not tell…

But whatever it was it did not matter.

After all, nothing mattered. She had to distance herself from everything that she was doing. Remember only *why* she was doing it. Because it was the only thing she could do that her mother wanted her to do. It didn't matter what anguish it caused her, she had to do it.

For her mother's sake.

Taking a deep, sharp breath, she gave a brief nod and went to the door to open it, to let him out again. She didn't want him in her bedroom.

She didn't want him anywhere near him.

It was much, much too dangerous.

But he didn't cross to the door. Instead he turned on his heel, walked out of the French windows onto the veranda, and disappeared to his right.

The thought that he could gain access to her room from the unlocked French windows made her suddenly nervous, and she hurried to where her handbag lay on the bed. The emeralds were still there.

Her mouth tightened. Vito Farneste would get them back—but not until his name was on her wedding certificate and his ring was on her finger.

In an hour and a half.

She went back into the bathroom to comb out her hair.

And adorn herself for her wedding.

CHAPTER SIX

THE sun was a molten orb cradled in crimson clouds. The sea was aflame with dark gold. The palm trees were etched against the burning sky like ebony statues. Music played from speakers hidden in the low vegetation.

Bach, thought Rachel, though she could not immediately identify the piece, familiar though it was.

But then her brain wasn't exactly working right now.

It took everything she had just to keep walking.

She walked very slowly. It was difficult to do anything else. The dress she was wearing, bought hurriedly the day before, and costing far more than she'd wanted to pay, was cut on the bias, in softest pale green satin, and shimmered along her body and spread out into a little demi-train. The bodice was softly folded, unadorned. But it needed no ornamentation.

The glittering green fire of the emeralds around her neck supplied that.

Fastening them around her throat had been difficult. Not because the catch was tricky, but because, as she'd lifted them out of their velvet bag and draped them around her, she had felt a terrible weight press down on her.

I've got no right to them! None! I'm not a Farneste bride! I'm an impostor, forcing myself on to my Farneste bridegroom.

Now, as she walked slowly through the warm, balmy air on her high-heeled sandals, towards the waiting group of people under a silk-swathed awning bathed in the rich light of the setting sun, she felt her skin prickle with superstitious dread.

For one long, crushing moment she thought of the last woman who had worn these emeralds as a Farneste bride. Vito's mother. The woman whose marriage vows her own mother had conspired to mock.

Consternation shook her. Accusing her.

I've no right to be here! No right to be doing this!

But she had to do it. She had to. The living, she knew, had an overwhelming obligation to the dying. Her mother had nothing left—nothing. Only a fevered, desperate fantasy to quiet her final months as her body yielded to its ultimate enemy.

I have no choice. I have to go through with it.

Her eyes rested on the group of people, getting closer as she approached them. Only one stood out—and not because of his white skin.

Vito Farneste. Waiting to marry her. His face like Carrara marble.

He was dressed in a black evening jacket, and he looked so devastating that Rachel could feel her stomach tighten. She had never seen him in a tuxedo, she realised, and she knew that the image would now be burnt onto her retinas for ever. He looked tall, and lean, and so breathtaking that all she could do was stare at him.

She tried not to, tried to drag her eyes away from him, to focus on the official who would conduct the ceremony, standing just to the side of a linen-draped table on which Rachel could see was a large, open leather-bound book.

But she only had eyes for Vito.

I'm mad! Mad to do this!

But it was too late for recriminations. Too late for regrets. She was going to marry Vito Farneste, make herself legally his wife, then go home to tell her dying mother that it was so.

And never see Vito again.

He was looking at her, she could tell. But his eyes gave

nothing away. As she got closer she found she could not meet them, and her gaze slipped away, towards the setting sun which streamed over the sea beyond the little arbour.

Again that sense of superstitious dread poured through her. It was as if by mocking such a fairytale setting for a wedding she was calling down on herself the curses of the gods.

For an instant, a terrible, brief moment, she let herself imagine how it might be if this were a real wedding, and she were in truth, as well as in law, a Farneste bride.

Then harsh words cut through her vision. Destructive, scathing. Scorning.

In your dreams...

Destroying all her hopes, as he had destroyed them once before.

She reached the arbour and paused. The cluster of Antillians—the celebrant, his assistant and two others, who were, Rachel assumed, there in the office of witnesses, plus, she was glad to see, a photographer with some formidable equipment to hand—all smartly clothed in dark suits were smiling away. The celebrant lifted his hands and opened his mouth to start the ceremony.

An air of total unreality settled over Rachel.

Then, before the celebrant could say anything, Vito spoke.

'One moment.' He turned his head to Rachel. 'You'll need to sign the pre-nup first. Or did you think I'd forget?'

The sardonic tone in his voice made her lips tighten. She said nothing, however, merely turned to where he was indicating with his left hand a document on the table beside the marriage register. It was the same document she'd read on the plane. She didn't bother to look at it again, simply turned to the last page and signed her name swiftly and carelessly. Then she straightened and went back to her place in front of the celebrant, who was looking studiedly blank about this invasion of harsh financial reality into this most romantic of wedding settings.

Vito addressed the two witnesses. 'If you wouldn't mind?' he prompted, and dutifully they put their names to the pre-nuptial contract that ensured Rachel would leave the marriage without a penny of Farneste money to her name.

Vito checked the signatures, and then went to stand beside his bride, his face expressionless.

My devoted and loving husband, thought Rachel, with a stab of viciousness.

Around her neck, the stones of the Farneste emeralds pressed with a dead weight, and for the first time she was glad to feel them there. Defiance flooded through her. She had no need to feel guilty! Vito Farneste had used and abused her seven years ago, destroying her innocence for the sake of his determination to wound her mother. That she was her mother's daughter was not her fault! It never had been! He had had no right to use her as his weapon.

And because of what he had done to her she had no need to feel compunction about what she was doing. The emeralds were her bride price, and they were buying for her a fine husband, all right!

A husband she would discard even faster than he could discard her!

Bitterness filled her, and through it piercing grief. She gazed blindly into the setting sun. An ocean away her mother lay in her hospital bed, filled with painkillers, her life ebbing away day by day.

The wedding ceremony began.

Words. She heard herself speaking them. Heard the celebrant. Heard the deep, Italian-accented tones of the man who stood beside her. Consenting to be her husband. Sliding his ring on her finger.

As the celebrant spoke the final declaration, making her

Vito's wife, she felt totally numb, as if liquid nitrogen had been poured along every vein in her body.

She did not hear the smiling, professional congratulations of the celebrant, or those of the two witnesses who added their anonymous signatures below hers and Vito's in the register and on the wedding certificate. She simply stood there, staring out over the sea where the last lip of the sun pencilled a line of gold along the horizon.

Feeling nothing.

Slowly she lifted her left hand and spread her fingers. There on her third finger gleamed the curving line of gold that Vito had placed there.

A flash made her blink. And then another. Surfacing, she realised that the photographer had started to take photographs.

She forced a smile to her mouth, trying to make herself look like a radiant bride. She needed photographs. Visual evidence to show her mother. Evidence that her daughter was, in truth, a Farneste bride, that Vito had done what his father had refused to do, what Vito himself had scorned to do even when he'd so callously parted her from her virginity and so cruelly dismissed her.

She stood beside him now, in this mockery of a wedding, smiling at the camera, hoping to God that Vito was not looking as if he were a spectre at the feast. Suddenly, on impulse, she found herself gazing up at him.

Her breath caught.

His face was impassive, and yet the kick to her guts was overwhelming. Her eyes distended, drinking him in, feasting on him.

And then suddenly, out of nowhere, he looked down at her.

Something blazed in his eyes, and it was like a whip of flame over her skin, scorching her.

For a second, an instant, she was enveloped in that flame, and then, like a conflagration, there was a flash.

But it was not her body igniting under that incredible scorching gaze.

It was the photographer catching the moment.

She jerked away from Vito, half stumbling forward. The ornate writing on the signed certificate caught her eye, and she turned to pick it up off the table. But Vito was before her. He folded it, slid it into his inside breast pocket. Rachel knew why. She wasn't going to be allowed to get her hands on it until Vito had his emeralds.

She stood stiffly while Vito turned his attention to the celebrant and his aides, thanking them for their offices. Then, as they took their leave, Rachel heard the soft pop of a champagne cork, and realised that a waiter had approached from the hotel with a tray bearing an ice bucket and two flutes.

He set his load down on the damask-draped table and proceeded to pour the champagne. It was the last thing Rachel wanted to do—stand here, under this flowery arbour, in the light of the setting sun, surrounded by tropical palms, and drink champagne. But the waiter was beaming at her as he offered her a brimming glass, and so she took it in nerveless fingers, trying to smile politely as the man offered his felicitations on her marriage. Then he was repeating the office for Vito, and finally leaving them both to it, with a last beaming smile, and heading back for the hotel.

Rachel watched him go. A sense of hideous tension seemed to net her. She took a sip of the icy liquid, feeling it effervesce on her tongue. Above the sea Venus rode low and luminous amongst the myriad pinpricks of stars.

Goddess of love, she thought acidly.

Again that sense of superstitious dread seemed to jitter through her, as though she had, with this travesty of a marriage, dangerously mocked the gods. Well, if she had, it was

too late now. Depression settled over her. She gazed out to
sea, sipping her champagne.

Eyes bleak.

Vito raised the champagne flute to his mouth, his eyes on
Rachel's profile. A sense of gutting disbelief cut through
him. He'd done it. He'd married her. Rachel Vaile. Arlene
Graham's daughter. For an instant he felt a kick in his guts,
as though he'd just done something quite irreversible.
Irreparable.

He pushed it aside. He'd known what he was doing, and
just because he'd now gone and done it, it changed nothing!
A civil marriage was not a sacrament. It was a legal transaction, nothing more. The certificate in his pocket made
Rachel Vaile his wife only in fact, not in truth. A fact that
could be reversed with another simple legal transaction.
Divorce.

All that brief, five-minute ceremony had accomplished
was to deliver Rachel Vaile into his hands.

Along with the Farneste emeralds.

His gaze shifted. They clung to her pale skin like living
green fire, and as he looked he felt that kick come again.

She had no right to them! No right at all. She was con-
taminating them with her touch, let alone her possession of
them! He should rip them from her throat!

And yet…

The kick came again.

She looked so perfect in them. The hard green jewels
graced her slender, swanlike neck, her throat, as if designed
for her and her alone.

How could she look so right in jewels that were never
meant for a woman of her kind?

His gaze slid upwards. His eyes narrowed.

The expression on her face was the same as it had been
on the plane, as she'd stared out of the porthole.

As bleak as winter's snow.

Something stabbed at him, some emotion he could not name. Almost he felt his hand reach out instinctively to touch her, resonate in some soundless, wordless sympathy.

And then, like a blade through his skull, he realised the cause of that bleak expression.

She was thinking of her lover! The man who would not marry her and whose rejection had stung her to get revenge on him for spurning her! That was why she was gazing with that lost, despairing look! Thinking of him. Yearning for him!

His expression hardened, a cold, cynical light entering his eye as he took another mouthful of champagne.

Before the night was over Rachel Vaile would have no thoughts for any man but himself! He was going to occupy her entire existence for the night—and as many nights after as he chose!

Rachel Vaile might be her mother's daughter, down to the last atom of her being, but that meant she'd inherited her mother's natural talent! He'd discovered that seven years ago, and now he would rediscover it. Taste it all again in the ripeness of her womanhood.

Whatever intentions to the contrary she might be arrogantly, foolishly entertaining.

Her scornful, insulting words to him seared in his brain.

'I know you think you're God's monumental gift to women, Vito, but I'm afraid so far as I'm concerned you're a bit of a yawn. I only wanted your ring on my finger, that's all. Not your stud services—magnificent as you consider them.'

His mouth twisted. By morning Rachel Vaile would be *begging* for his stud services.

Gagging for them.

It was all she deserved from him.

*   *   *

Rachel took another sip of the champagne. There was no point feeling bad about what she had done. She just had to keep going, count the hours until she was back in London and could get to the hospital to tell her mother the glad tidings…

She felt her lips twist. Glad tidings? Forcing a man to marry her who loathed her, whom she loathed?

Involuntarily her head turned slightly towards the man standing only a few feet away from her—and yet a world away. In the tropical dusk his skin tone seemed darker, his features edged with shadow.

Like *chiaroscuro*. Light and dark.

Just like Vito himself. But the light was fake, all fake. Only the darkness in him was real.

Again, those two lines from that most bitter of all Shakespeare sonnets haunted her.

For I have sworn thee fair and thought thee bright
Who art as black as hell, as dark as night.

She knew—dear God, she knew!—what had driven the poet to write those lines.

I can't stand this, she thought. It's agony. Exquisite agony.

She took a deep, unsteady breath and deliberately, determinedly, swallowed a large mouthful of champagne. Her feelings for Vito Farneste were a total irrelevance.

With a sharp movement she put her champagne glass down on the table. Her hands went to the back of her neck. As she fiddled with the clasp of the necklace, trying to get her fingers into position on it, she twisted her head towards Vito.

She must be brisk about this. Brisk, efficient, emotionless.

This was, after all, a business transaction—nothing more, despite the beauty of the island, the deliberate romanticism of the setting. Whatever she had once felt for Vito was dead. Killed outright in the moment he'd got out of that bed and informed her mother she'd been gagging for it...

Deliberately she forced the vile memory to the front of her mind. It would give her the courage to keep going. To ignore the fact that Vito Farneste was here, in the flesh, looking more breathtaking than she had ever seen him, the sight of him churning through her, devastating her.

She spoke tersely. 'As soon as you have the emeralds I want the certificate.' There was an edge to her voice she did not bother to soften.

'Don't take them off!'

Astonishment made her pause, hands stilling at her nape. 'Why not?' she demanded.

He gave a smile. 'The night is young, *cara mia*.'

She gazed at him warily. What was going on?

'What's that supposed to mean?' she countered, her hands lowering slowly.

'It means that I believe we are awaited for dinner.'

He cocked his head towards the hotel.

'I'm not hungry.'

Something glimmered in his eye. 'But I am. And besides, you need food to keep your strength up. And to keep your *bella figura*.' His gaze flickered over her.

It felt like fire, licking at her.

He was doing it on purpose, she knew.

'Stop it!' she said sharply. 'Vito, what the hell do you think you're doing? If I'm hungry I'll order room service. You can eat in the dining room if you want.'

He shook his head.

'Uh-uh. No deal.' His eyes rested on her. 'We've aroused quite enough suspicions as it is by our attitude. After all...' his voice took on a caustic note '...we are hardly behaving as the typical romantic couple, are we? And although Antillian law permits instant weddings, it likes them to be genuine ones. Antillia doesn't want to get a reputation for tolerating false marriages for legally dubious purposes.' His eyes glinted. He was clearly enjoying her discomfort. 'Which means we do our best to behave in a manner calculated to set their minds at rest about us. By indulging in a candlelit romantic dinner *à deux*.'

She felt colour flush along her cheekbones at his words. She knew he was baiting her, and that she should not react, but she coloured all the same.

'Well, why can't we both have room service, then?' she countered.

He shrugged. 'If you prefer, *cara mia*. Though, of course, to avoid arousing suspicions about us we would need to dine together, in the privacy of our suite, completely *à deux*...'

The baiting look came again, and her mouth thinned.

'Very well. We'll dine in the dining room. I'll go and change.'

She spoke shortly and made to turn. A hand reached out and stayed her. She froze. She didn't want Vito touching her. Not anywhere.

'A bride should always dine in her wedding gown—and with all her finery.'

Again his gaze swept over her, and again the colour flared out along her cheekbones.

'I'd have thought you'd want me to take off the emeralds as soon as possible!' she bit back. 'That's why you just married me after all! To get them back!'

Something lit in his eye, and she knew she had touched a nerve.

'I'll take them off later,' he replied. 'Do you doubt it?'

Her lips pressed together.

'No. And in exchange I want the wedding certificate. It's all I want from you!'

That light came into his eye again, and she felt the blood in her veins swirl in disturbing little eddies. It must be the champagne, she thought.

It couldn't be anything else.

It mustn't be.

As they headed back along the path to the hotel, Vito strolling beside her as if, she thought with stinging animosity, he had not a care in the world, half-full champagne bottle swinging gently from his fingers, she found memories stealing through her mind. Unwanted memories. Memories of Vito strolling through the dusk across the Roman Forum. Walking through time, he'd told her. And they'd tried to imagine themselves as ancient Romans, and all the sights and sounds that would have been around them, to rebuild in their imaginations the buildings they were passing.

Talking together. Laughing together. Being together.

Pain laced through her at the memories.

I thought we were so close.

But it was fake. All fake.

As fake, she knew, some minutes later, as Vito's solicitous attitude to her now.

She was ushered up the shallow wooden steps onto the wide veranda that ran the whole length of the front of the hotel.

Last time it was me he was fooling—this time it's just the hotel staff and guests.

She walked through the double doors into a beautiful high-ceilinged, mahogany-panelled dining room.

Speaking of guests…where were they?

There was only one table in the dining room, groaning with silverware and crystal, lit by candles floating in a beautiful silver bowl at the centre, in which fragrant petals floated. The whole bowl was surrounded by a beautiful floral arrangement. A single red rose rested by one of the two place settings.

An Important Message from the Editors

Dear Reader,

If you'd enjoy reading romance novels with larger print that's easier on your eyes, let us send you *TWO FREE HARLEQUIN INTRIGUE® NOVELS* in our *NEW LARGER-PRINT EDITION.* These books are complete and unabridged, but the type is set about 25% bigger to make it easier to read. Look inside for an actual-size sample.

By the way, you'll also get a surprise gift with your two free books!

Pam Powers

Peel off Seal and Place Inside...

LARGER-PRINT
FREE BOOKS
EDITION

THE RIGHT WOMAN

she'd thought she was fine. It took Daniel's words and Brooke's question to make her realize she was far from a full recovery.

She'd made a start with her sister's help and she intended to go forward now. Sarah felt as if she'd been living in a darkened room and someone had suddenly opened a door, letting in the fresh air and sunshine. She could feel its warmth slowly seeping into the coldest part of her. The feeling was liberating. She realized it was only a small step and she had a long way to go, but she was ready to face life again with Serena and her family behind her.

All too soon, they were saying goodbye and Sarah experienced a moment of sadness for all the years she and Serena had missed. But they had each other now and th t's what

She held asy o

YOURS FREE!
*You'll get a great mystery gift with
your two free larger-print books!*

The Harlequin Reader Service™ — Here's How It Works:

Accepting your 2 free Harlequin Intrigue® larger-print books and gift places you under no obligation to buy anything. You may keep the books and gift and return the shipping statement marked "cancel." If you do not cancel, about a month later we'll send you 6 additional Harlequin Intrigue larger-print books and bill you just $4.49 each in the U.S., or $5.24 each in Canada, plus 25¢ shipping & handling per book and applicable taxes if any.* That's the complete price and — compared to cover prices of $5.24 each in the U.S. and $6.24 each in Canada — it's quite a bargain! You may cancel at any time, but if you choose to continue, every month we'll send you 6 more books, which you may either purchase at the discount price or return to us and cancel your subscription.

*Terms and prices subject to change without notice. Sales tax applicable in N.Y. Canadian residents will be charged applicable provincial taxes and GST.

If offer card is missing write to: Harlequin Reader Service, 3010 Walden Ave., P.O. Box 1867, Buffalo, NY 14240-1867

BUSINESS REPLY MAIL
FIRST-CLASS MAIL   PERMIT NO. 717-003   BUFFALO, NY

POSTAGE WILL BE PAID BY ADDRESSEE

HARLEQUIN READER SERVICE
3010 WALDEN AVE
PO BOX 1867
BUFFALO NY 14240-9952

NO POSTAGE
NECESSARY
IF MAILED
IN THE
UNITED STATES

For a second so brief it was hardly there Rachel remembered her dream on the plane—running up the Spanish Steps in Rome, a street vendor proffering a single red rose.

Memory fused with the dream. Memory of being utterly, incandescently happy, secure in the knowledge that the most beautiful man in the world had singled her out, had sought her company, taken her to his bed.

Oh, God, I was such a fool…

Someone was gliding towards them—the white-gloved butler, André, beaming with pleasure and ushering them to the table.

Rachel stalled.

'I don't want a private dining room,' she announced baldly. 'I want to be in the main dining room, please.'

The man looked confused. A voice behind Rachel spoke, dry and accented.

'There is no main dining room, *cara mia.*'

She frowned. 'So do the other hotel guests all have private dining rooms?' she asked, bewildered.

'Other guests?' echoed André. 'Madam—there are no other guests. This is not a hotel. It is a villa that your husband has hired—Honeymoon House.'

Rachel stared, then twisted around towards Vito.

'There's nobody else here?'

But she didn't need an answer—she knew it was true. This was some kind of private house set up to arrange weddings for couples rich enough to have the place to themselves. She opened her mouth to protest—she could not stay here, all on her own with Vito and no other guests—then shut it again as she saw the warning light in his eye, reminding her not to arouse suspicions. Stiffly she took the seat being held for her, and allowed the butler to deferentially shake out the pristine white linen table napkin and lay it across her lap, then go to perform the same office for Vito.

There followed a whirl of highly professional, superbly executed activity, as their champagne glasses were refilled, a carafe of iced water was placed on the table, warmed bread rolls were presented to them in a silver filigree basket, with curls of butter in iced water dishes, and salvers of tiny, delicious-looking crudités were proffered. A silver-printed menu card was placed in front of Rachel, and one in front of Vito, and she gazed at the ornate embossing of wedding bells and hearts surrounding the copperplate descriptions of the meal ahead. For his part, Vito was in deep discussion with André over a leather-bound wine list.

Clearly the staff were determined that this was going to be a wedding night dinner to beat all others hands down.

A sense of complete unreality settled over Rachel. This might be the world's most hypocritical meal, but there was nothing she could do about it. As her second glass of champagne slipped down her throat she felt a blessed sense of dissociation float over her. The ordeal of the wedding was over—whenever she moved her fork, the gold of her wedding ring glinted in the candlelight.

It's done. I can relax now. Nothing can undo what has been achieved. I've carried out my mother's dying wish and I can be content.

Little by little she felt the strain begin to ease from her shoulders. It was as if the heavy, crushing burden that she had been carrying was slipping from her. There was no need to carry it any longer. She could let it slide to the ground.

The net of tension that had been wound so tightly around her began to dissolve.

I feel free, she thought. And it seemed a wondrous, strange idea.

As she ate the delicious food washed down by the rich, expensive wine, the last of the tension slipped from her.

She wasn't sure how, but somehow the meal passed more easily than she could have dreamt possible. Because of the hovering attendance of the staff Vito made a point of making innocuous conversation with her, and although her replies were stilted and awkward she realised it was all only for show, and therefore meant nothing.

The wine helped too, and there seemed to be a lot of it. After the champagne white wine was served with seafood, then a vintage red with the lamb, and sweet wine with the dessert.

And all the time, as the tension dissolved away from her with every mouthful of wine, so her heightened awareness of Vito's presence mounted.

She tried hard not to look at him, but her eyes kept going to him. Never to meet his gaze openly, but just tiny, irresistible flickers that caught glimpses of him, time after time. She knew she should not, understand she was being insanely foolish, and yet the knowledge that after tonight she would never set eyes on him again for the rest of her life was piercing.

A slow, terrible yearning began to run through her like a silent, flowing river, cutting through the levees of resistance she had constructed so uselessly to contain the flooding of wanting, yearning. Desiring.

I want him so much. And I can never have him. Never. After tonight there will be nothing...

Vito let his gaze flicker over the woman sitting opposite him. Her awareness of him had been growing throughout the long meal. She might be trying to suppress it, but she could not conceal it from him. The covert looks from beneath those long, beautiful lashes licked over him, increasing not just her awareness of him, but his of her.

He wanted her badly.

And he wanted her to want him even more.

That would be exquisitely satisfying. As satisfying as sinking deep, deep within that satined flesh.

He felt his own flesh respond even at the thought of what was yet to come, so soon now, and reached for his wine glass to distract himself. The meal was nearing its end, and he was glad of it. Because, for him, the night was only just beginning.

CHAPTER SEVEN

RACHEL rested her hands on the balustrade of the veranda and gazed out into the warm Caribbean night. She could hear the soft soughing of the sea breeze in the palm tops, and the faint susurration of the waves breaking gently on the beach. Her eyes adjusted to the night and she began to make out shapes, shadows. The moon rode high in the heavens.

A night for lovers, she thought.

But not for her.

A sense of exile overcame her. She could stand here, in these beautiful, fairytale surroundings, and not be here at all. It was as if everything around her were real and she was not.

The wine in her veins made her feel even more distanced from the reality around her.

She tried to think of her mother, tried to work out what time it must be in London now. To think of what the doctors were telling her now—that it was time to start thinking of hospice care for her mother...

But her mother seemed very far away.

Only here, now, seemed real.

And yet she was not part of this beautiful romantic setting. Could never be. The one man she wanted—had ever wanted—was beyond her reach.

That he was here, now, in the flesh, a few metres away from her, only made her anguish more exquisite, her torment more painful. It didn't matter whether Vito Farneste were ten metres from her or ten thousand miles—she did not exist for him.

101

Had never existed.

I should go to bed. Go to sleep.

And pray not to dream...

She would go in a moment. Just a moment.

She lifted her face a little. The fresh, sweet breeze played over her cheeks, lifting a few delicate strands of hair loose from her chignon, moving along her bare arms and shoulders.

That terrible, anguished sense of longing swept over her again, of wanting so much, so *much*, something that could never be. The ache, welling through her whole body, seemed to consume her utterly.

There was a soft footfall behind her.

And a presence.

A presence she would recognise blindfolded and in the depths of a cavern. A presence she was so attuned to that her whole body vibrated subliminally to it.

She turned. She could not help it.

And he was there. As beautiful as when she had first set eyes on him, his face limned by shadow.

She stood, backed against the balustrade, and all she could hear was the beat of her heart.

He moved towards her. She felt the breath catch in her throat. Her eyes widened. He was coming towards her.

Purpose in his tread.

She couldn't move. Not a muscle. Her whole existence seemed suspended, floating in insubstantiality.

And yet she had never been more aware of her body in her life. She could feel her gown grazing along her hips, her legs, feel the soft swell of her breasts against its satin folds. Feel the blood pulse slowly, languorously, in her veins.

Her heartbeat slowed.

He came up to her.

She gazed at him. She could not help it. Eyes drinking him in. So beautiful.

Why was he coming to her? What did he want?

For a brief, singing moment she thought that he was intent on her—*her*—as he once had been. So many years ago. To touch her, kiss her, caress her and possess her...

Her lips parted.

He smiled.

A wry, knowing smile. The long lashes of his eyes swept down, grazing her mouth as if he had already kissed her.

He would kiss her now, she knew—any moment he would lower his head to hers and take her lips with his...

Yearning filled her. Yearning and wanting and desiring.

'Vito...' She breathed his name, her eyes beseeching.

He reached out a hand.

He would cup her cheek, fold her to him, embrace her...

But all he did was let his forefinger rest on the pendant emerald nestling almost in the valley of her breasts.

'Time to give me the emeralds, *cara mia*.'

There was amusement in his voice. Even as he spoke his other hand reached into his jacket pocket, withdrawing the folded marriage certificate.

'You give me the emeralds, I give you this,' he told her. His eyes were dark in the night. They played over her face.

Her stricken, anguished face.

He looked down at her.

'This is what we came here for, no? To make this trade? There was no other reason, was there, *cara mia*?'

The smile on his mouth mocked her pain. Her yearning.

Her eyes were full. Agonised.

'Give me the necklace,' he said softly.

He dropped his hand away.

She felt her hands move numbly, as if they were no part of her, reaching to the nape of her neck. The clasp gave way in her fingers and she felt the weight of the emeralds slide from her. She caught them in a pool of darkness, cupping them in her hands. She held them out to him.

He took them from her and slid them into his jacket pocket. Then, never taking his eyes from her face, he folded the wedding certificate into a thin column and slipped it into her bodice, between her breasts.

'You have what you came for, *cara mia*.' His voice was still low. 'Because that is *all* you came here for—nothing else.' For one long, endless moment he let his eyes hold hers. 'Nothing else,' he repeated softly. Then his finger slid under her chin and tilted it up. 'You did not come for this, did you?'

His mouth lowered to hers, brushing it like silk.

Heaven sighed through her.

He lifted his mouth away.

'Or this?'

His fingers slid around her throat, to cup the back of her head. And then once again he lowered his mouth to hers.

She could not move, could not breathe. Could only stand there while Vito kissed her, opening her mouth and letting the honey within sweeten the moment to exquisite bliss.

It seemed to her that his kiss lasted for ever—and yet for only the briefest moment. As he drew back from her she gave a soft, anguished cry of loss.

He looked down at her. His eyes were dark, dark as the night that embraced them both.

'What do you want?' he asked, and his voice was soft and low.

She reached to touch his face with her fingers, trace the contours of his jaw, his chin, his beautiful, sinful mouth. Tempting her beyond endurance.

'I want you,' she breathed.

He smiled. The smile of a fallen angel.

'Then you shall have me, *cara mia*. You shall have me.'
He led her away, to his bed, and she went with him.

At the threshold to his room he paused, and with a sudden
sweep lifted her into his arms and carried her inside. As he
lowered her down on his bed she gasped.

The bed was circular. Circular and vast. Swathed in white
satin, piled high with the softest cushions. Overhead white
muslin bunched like a gathered veil, which could be loosened to give them absolute privacy.

He looked down at her, lying there in green satin on the
huge bed.

'Welcome to the honeymoon suite, *cara mia*,' he said
softly.

For a moment, just a brief, fleeing moment, a sense of
dread so great came over her that she felt as if someone had
just walked over her grave.

She was no bride. Not in any truth she knew of. She had
no right to be here.

Then her eyes came back to rest on Vito, his hands reaching for his neck and loosening his evening tie.

She could only watch as the sliver of black fell to the
floor, as the black jacket of his tuxedo was removed, tossed
carelessly on a padded chair, as his fingers swiftly, silently,
undid the buttons of his dress shirt.

To reveal the smooth, lean perfection that lay beneath.

She was lost, completely lost. She could not move, could
not do anything except lie there supine, helpless, while Vito
removed his clothes.

And all the while he looked down at her, his eyes holding
her still for him as he readied himself for her.

Naked, he came to sit on the side of the bed, and reached
for the strap of her dress. He slid it from her shoulder, and then
repeated the task with the other strap. And then, with slow
deliberation, he drew down the bodice to reveal her breasts.

They peaked beneath his gaze, and for one long, endless moment she simply stared at him, letting him look at her. Then in a murmured breath she exhaled his name—and her desire.

'Vito—please…'

Slowly, very slowly, he lowered his mouth to her breast.

And as he did so the folded paper between her breasts fell to the floor unnoticed. Unregarded. Unimportant.

'Vito…' Her breath was a sigh, an imprecation, an invocation. An invocation to all that held her bliss in the world. Vito Farneste, who was making love to her again.

Her body knew him. Knew his body. She took him into her. Felt the strong, swift thrust of his body into hers. Cried out at his possession. And cried again, higher and yet higher, as he caressed her with smoothing hands and melting lips and delicate, skilful fingers that knew how to touch, to stroke, to draw from her every drop of sweetness.

And the sweetest of all the bliss that was possessing her was the knowledge that she had Vito back again. Vito as he had been that night, that precious, wonderful, magical night, when he had made a woman of her.

And, as she had that night, so again this night she gave her body to him and all her being—arching towards him, embracing him, yielding to him all that she was, all that she had to give.

His touch was honey and fire and licking, flickering flame, playing over her skin, inflaming it, reaching every inch of her, every secret place, setting her alight, aflame. Her mouth clung to his, her body to his, cleaving and clasping, holding him to her, closer and more closely still, her hands desperate to catch him back with every slow, withdrawing thrust, pulling him in again to her, as the flame burned in her veins, her throat, her mouth, the very core of her being.

He lifted her hands above her head, fastening them with

his strong, flexing arms, moving his lean, powerful body with slow, relentless strokes. She could feel the flame turn to the first exquisite flickerings of pleasure growing with each thrust, caressing the very heart of her, until she felt the flickerings merge and meld into a sweet, hot pool of liquid flame that brimmed almost, *almost*, to overflowing.

But not quite…not quite.

Her body arched to his, hips lifting, imploring, her mouth catching at his, her lips soft and desperate.

'Vito…' His name was a breath, an exhalation, a plea.

He stilled, and his very stillness was agony to her.

'Vito…' she breathed again.

He lifted his mouth from hers and gazed down at her. The planes of his face were thrown into stark contrast by the low, glowing light of the soft lamp.

She drank him in like the sweetest wine, the most beautiful man in the world, making love to her…

For one long, timeless moment he looked back at her, and she could see the dark shade of passion in his eyes.

Passion. Passion for her. For her alone.

Time seemed to stop, the universe seemed to stop, everything that had ever existed, ever could exist, seemed to stop, and she was caught here, now, for ever, on the very lip of bliss.

Then slowly, with infinite control, he stroked deep, deep within her, one last, final time.

The pool of fire at her body's core brimmed…and overflowed.

Like lava spilling through her veins the sweet, unbearable excitement spread out in pulse after undulating pulse of hot, pouring pleasure, suffusing through every cell, every atom of her body, flowing through her limbs.

She cried out, a high, unearthly sound, her eyes fluttering closed as her whole being became the sensation pouring through her.

And even as her hips strained upwards, the burning tension in her muscles only accentuating the sheet of flame that lit her body like a torch, she felt him move again. Not slow, not controlled, but urgent, hungry, devouring.

She felt his body convulse into hers, and it was her ecstasy too. She cried out again, her head thrashing, heels digging into the bedclothes, as her body bowed upward to his.

And still the lava poured through her body, an endless, unstoppable welling of sensation that went on and on, so that she was all that it was, and it was all that she was.

Until with one final powerful pulse his surging peaked, and suddenly the weight of his body was pressing down on her, spent, exhausted, sated.

His hands slackened on hers and she felt his weight on her hips, extinguishing the last eddies of the fire that had consumed her. She was shaken to her core, her breathing ragged, rasping.

She gazed up at him, her eyes blank with wonder, heart pounding in her chest, her body slick with sweat.

He looked down at her. She could see the feathering of his hair, damp on his forehead, the stark etching of his cheekbones, the straining cords of his throat. For a moment—timeless, endless—she could not speak or move, could only gaze, and gaze, and gaze.

Vito—Vito—had made love to her. Had taken her back to that place where she had dared not go, even in her dreams, and now she was there again, in his arms, his bed.

It was going to be all right. She knew it with a deep, abiding certainty. How she knew she did not understand, but the truth, the strength of what had just happened could not be denied. The poisoned past was gone now, burned out in the flame of passion shared.

She gazed up at him, her breath still ragged, her body

still shaken to its extremity by what she had just experienced.

With a slow, leisurely movement Vito lowered his head to brush her lips. She could not kiss him back. Exhaustion drained her and she lay passive, supine.

As he lifted his head from her he smiled.

And in that moment, as he spoke, the breath stopped in her throat.

'You must let me know, *cara mia*, when you want my stud services again. If you promise to respond to me like that again you shall have them any time you want...'

His voice was low and mocking.

She felt the blood drain from her body and a chill, numbing horror take its place in her veins.

He raised himself from her, releasing her hands. He drew one long, insolent finger along her cheek.

'You've improved a lot since you were eighteen—that lover of yours must be good. He's taught you well. You should give him my compliments. Tell him how much I appreciated his tuition of you.'

She heard him speak but could say nothing. Could only lie there while the horror drenched through her.

He drew out of her, his naked body glistening with sweat in the dim light.

For one long, horror-stricken second she stared at him. At the absolute perfection of muscle and sinew that was the body of Vito Farneste.

A fallen angel's body.

With a fallen angel's soul.

He got to his feet and looked down at her.

'I need a shower. Do you care to join me? It could be very...reviving...'

He reached down as if to touch her.

She ran. Ran as if all the devils in hell were after her. Or just one ruined, fallen angel. Stumbling to her feet, she ran like a wounded, desperate thing, to gain the sanctuary of her own room along the veranda.

The French windows opened to her desperate tugging and she slammed them shut behind her, fumbling for the lock.

Then, with a stricken, broken cry, she threw herself onto the bed, burying deep within the covers as though it was her grave.

She lay, legs drawn up, sideways, in a protective, instinctive foetal position, her head and arms buckled inwards, hunched and bowed.

She could not even cry.

Vito stared down at the empty bed. There was an emptiness inside him and he did not know why.

He had, after all, done exactly what he had intended. He had taken Rachel Vaile to bed again and enjoyed every ounce of her seasoned ripeness.

And made very, very sure that she enjoyed him too.

That, after all, had been the whole purpose of this farce. To wipe from her face that mocking, scornful, *lying* contempt of him!

Well, he had proved it a lie, all right! *Dio*, with every stroke of his body she had flamed for him!

And I for her…

His mouth tightened angrily. Well, why should he not have? Rachel Vaile could arouse any man.

But then, that had always been true.

Ever since the second time he had set eyes on her.

Memory flashed in his brain.

She had been standing there, quite lost-looking in that sea of people, her hair like a pale golden veil. As he had approached her, instinctively drawn to her, he had realised how young she was.

And in the moment he had first stopped in front of her and smiled he had realised how untouched she was.

And how much he wanted to touch her.

He snapped the memory off. What the hell was the point in remembering Rachel?

Then or now.

With an impatient gesture he threw back the bedclothes, lowering his body onto the bed.

Immediately he felt her absence, and it stabbed at him like a knife.

He wanted her again. He wasn't nearly done with her.

But he wouldn't fetch her yet. He would leave her lying in the room next door, facing up to the fact that, however much she might deny it, however much she might tell him that she was immune to him, however much she might only have wanted his ring on her finger to flaunt in the face of a lover who had rejected her, Rachel Vaile was *his* for the taking.

And always would be!

He lay gazing up at the froth of white muslin overhead. Then, irritated by its reminder that this was supposed to be the honeymoon suite, he reached out and snapped off the bedside lamp, letting the night surge around him with only the muted hum of the air-conditioning around him. Though sated, his body felt restless, unquiet. His mind was stormy. Disturbed. And the very fact that it was in such a condition was itself unsettling. There was no reason for it. He had got exactly what he'd wanted. Everything that Rachel had to offer him.

Her sensuous, sensual body.

Because he'd learnt, seven long years ago, that that was all there was to Rachel that he could possibly ever want.

The rest had just been an illusion.

A cruel, hollow illusion.

He lay, eyes hard, and stared blindly into the dark.

* * *

Reaching for her toothbrush, Rachel realised that her hand was shaking. She tried to steady it, but it would not be still. She picked up the tube of toothpaste, held it to the toothbrush and squeezed out a pea-sized amount.

The strong mint flavour burned her mouth, but it also burnt away the stale sourness of last night's alcohol. She wished it could burn away last night as well.

Don't think. Don't think. Whatever you do, don't think.

She repeated the words like a mantra in her mind as she scrubbed with shaking viciousness at her teeth.

I knew. I knew what he was. I've known for seven long, bitter years. I have no excuse, none whatsoever. None.

How could he have changed from what she knew him to be?

But I wanted him to have changed! I wanted to be wrong about him! I wanted to believe in him…

She had wanted him to be the man she had once, so long ago, thought him to be. But he never had been. He had been an illusion.

A cruel, hollow illusion.

And last night he had conjured that illusion again, and once again he had deceived her with it. As easily as he had the first time.

But this time she did not even have the excuse of inexperienced youth. Or ignorance of his true nature.

She stared at her reflection, remorseless, unforgiving.

You deserve everything you got. Everything.

Loathing flowed through her. Not just for him, but for herself, her stupidity.

She started to pack away her toiletries, swiftly, methodically, unthinkingly. Then she realised she had not yet showered, left her toilet bag on the unit and stepped inside the cubicle.

Deliberately, self-hatingly, she turned the dial to cold, wanting to punish her flesh for having so beguiled her. Betrayed her.

But the water only came out tepid in these climes. She let it pound over her, wanting it to pummel her to the floor, wanting to feel its stinging needles mortify her skin. But instead she felt her body quiver in sensate awareness. She took the shower gel and rubbed it roughly over her body, wanting to slough it from her. But it only foamed and creamed beneath her palms, rich and luxuriating.

Arousing…

She rinsed abruptly and stepped out of the shower, seizing a towel to scour her skin with. But it was deep, and soft, and comforting.

She thrust it aside.

There was no comfort. None to be found. Not for her folly.

Only emptiness and devastation.

As she walked back into the bedroom she looked out over the gardens. It must be very early morning; the sun was only just above the horizon behind the house. She wondered how soon any of the staff would be stirring, so that she could summon transport from the island and back to the airport. She dressed swiftly, throwing on the same outfit in which she'd arrived, and packed the rest of her clothes. Her wedding dress was not there. She didn't care. Never wanted to set eyes on it again. It was contaminated. She closed down the lid of the small valise, fastened it, and froze in hideous realisation.

She did not have her marriage certificate. Vito had slid it between her breasts when he started his process of seduction. It must have fallen when he'd removed her dress.

Dismay surged through her in sickening waves.

I can't! I can't go back in there to get it! I can't!

But it was what she had come here for. The sole purpose of this whole vile nightmare. She had to go and get it. She had no choice.

On leaden, dread-filled steps she crossed to the French

windows, turning the key in the lock and carefully, cautiously, opening them. She stepped out onto the terrace. The cool of early morning washed over her, and without intent her gaze drifted out over the gardens.

And stilled.

Someone was in the pool. Swimming. Long, rhythmic strokes that ploughed up the water.

A sudden surge of opportunity struck her, and she twisted her head to the right. The doors of the honeymoon suite stood open.

It had to be Vito in the pool. It just had to be! Not even daring to think, Rachel dashed into the room, her eyes darting round fearfully. It was deserted—the huge circular bed empty, bedclothes on the floor. She averted her eyes as heat surged in her body.

Heat and mortification.

No time! No time for that! Time only to scour the floor in a desperate search for that single folded piece of paper.

I've got to find it! I've got to!

She could see nothing on the floor, and with deepest reluctance, but driven by an urgency she had to obey, she started to search the bed itself.

Don't think—just look!

It was there! Bundled up in the bedclothes. Crumpled, but—she unfolded it fumblingly—still legible and undefaced. She knelt up, scanning the page, making sure it was still all right.

'Why, *cara mia*, have I been keeping you waiting and now you come in search of me? You are eager to resume our pleasures, I can see.'

Vito was standing there at the open French windows, in nothing but bathing trunks. His body glistened damply, his hair was silky with water, and a towel was thrown over one shoulder. Along the line of his jaw she could see an early-morning shadow darkening his skin.

Rachel felt her insides hollow out, cutting through the horror at having been intercepted before she could fly.

She slid one leg to the floor and stood up, facing him, rapidly folding the certificate. She felt as if a bomb had exploded inside her guts, but she knew she must not show it. Must not.

Her face was tight, her voice barely controlled.

'This was all I came for, Vito.' She held up the certificate. Her voice was taut, barely controlled.

He strolled into the room. He looked relaxed, but Rachel could see that tension was racking through him.

She saw too, her eyes sucked to him, the smooth perfection of his torso, every ab and pec lovingly moulded, the superb masculine grace of his shoulders, his lean, narrow hips, his long muscled legs…

She dragged her eyes away, but there was nowhere safe to look. Nowhere. His face, cheekbones stark, eyes like dark, glinting pools, were just as dangerous to her.

He approached the bed, talking again.

'Are you telling me that my stud services are not up to your demanding standard? You seemed happy enough with them last night.'

He rested his dark eyes on her face. She felt the breath freeze in her lungs, her heart slow to a halt.

'You loved it last night,' he said softly, and a wave of nausea went through her. 'You couldn't get enough of it! You were begging for it!' He walked towards her, his eyes never leaving hers. '*Gagging* for it.' He tossed the towel aside and came towards her, purpose in every stride, a light in her eyes that made her stomach churn. 'And you'll love it again—you'll be begging me for it. Pleading. You'll be gagging for it again…'

He stopped in front of her, his hand coming up to reach for her.

She jerked away.

'You bastard!' Her voice was a whisper, a hoarse exhalation from her lungs. 'You vile, disgusting bastard! How dare you say such things to me? How *dare* you?'

Something flared in his eyes. His mouth was like a whip.

'That show of virtuous outrage didn't wash seven years ago, *cara mia*—and it doesn't wash now! So spare me the histrionics this time around. There's no need for them. This time around you've got my ring on your finger—the ring you've wanted ever since you schemed with your precious mother all those years ago! Setting you up as bait to catch me with! Little Miss Innocent—straight out of the schoolroom! But ready to open your legs for a chance to catch yourself a rich husband!'

The blood drained from Rachel's face.

'What…what do you mean…setting me up…?'

Vito's eyes narrowed contemptuously.

'Don't take me for a fool! You set me up, didn't you? Sweet eighteen and never been kissed! Pretty as a picture and just as untouched! And as corrupt and scheming as your mother! Your doting, oh-so-protective mother, who just *happened* to arrive back with my father that morning, just in oh-so-convenient time to find her darling virginal daughter deflowered by her protector's son! And she really thought, didn't she—and you too!—that my father would actually expect me to marry you because of it? Because I'd taken your virginity. The virginity so carefully guarded and then offered up in the hope of such fantastic financial gain! Marriage to a Farneste! What the mother could not achieve, the daughter would achieve for her…'

Faintness pulled at Rachel, swirling around her like a thickening mist.

'And now you've done it, haven't you? Achieved your

goal! Got yourself a Farneste for a husband! Your virginity might not have been currency enough, but the Farneste emeralds did the trick, didn't they? No wonder your mother decided to sacrifice them in such a noble cause! Her daughter's marriage to me! Second time lucky... Only this time around you thought you'd short-change me, didn't you? Sex didn't work to trap me seven years ago, so this time you pulled it from the menu! I wasn't even going to get your body to enjoy this time around, was I? That cheap, vindictive little denial was going to be your revenge, wasn't it? Your revenge for my refusal to marry you in the past. Wasn't it? *Wasn't it?*'

There was a flame in his eyes. A dark, burning flame.

'You were going to hold out on me. Taunt me with that beautiful body of yours and then cheat me of it! Well, *cara mia*, you miscalculated with that ambitious little brain of yours! You underestimated your own carnal appetite. You want me every time I touch you! You go up in flames for me! So don't lie to me! Don't try to tell me you don't want me! What did it take last night to get you into my bed? One touch, one kiss—and you were there! You couldn't get enough of me! You wanted me last night and you want me now!'

He shifted his weight to his other leg.

'Now, I'm off to take a shower, and then we'll have breakfast. Don't even think of trying to run—because, as I told you last night, I don't want any accusations thrown at me that I've entered into a fraudulent marriage. We are going to spend our honeymoon here, *cara mia*—our delightful, romantic honeymoon. You, my lovely bride, can have all you want of me! And I am going to enjoy the one thing I know you're good for!'

He turned and walked into the *en suite* bathroom, shutting the door behind him with a hollow thud.

Rachel swayed. Her legs were like cottonwool.

How could he have turned the truth on its head like that? Twisted his infamy of seven years ago so that *he* was the one who looked hard-done-by? The injured party, victim of a plot to trap him into marriage.

She felt winded, punched by what he had thrown at her. He had turned everything that he had done to her—knowingly, deliberately, calculatedly and remorselessly—upside down and inside out. Making *her* out to be the scheming, manipulative villain of the piece!

'You bastard,' she whispered, her lips hardly moving. 'You total, total bastard, to try and put the blame on me!'

Rage started to curl through her, filling up her lungs so that she could hardly breathe, misting in front of her vision. She shut her eyes and felt the rage trembling through her.

Between her legs she felt the dull, throbbing ache that had been there since she'd surfaced from her tormented sleep.

She'd felt that pain once before, and though it had been sharper then it had been nothing to the agony that had followed afterwards. The agony of knowing that Vito Farneste, who had murmured sweet nothings to her, smiled at her and laughed with her, who had taken her to heaven in his arms, who had bestowed his fabulous, beautiful body upon her and made a woman of her, had only been conducting a deliberate exercise in wounding the woman he hated.

That agony of her heart had been far, far worse than any pain from the physical parting with her virginity.

She opened her eyes, looking through the lens of seven long, long years.

I never got rid of the agony, she thought. Never. It's still there, deep inside. Festering, poisoning my life…

What did I think? she wondered. That Vito might some day feel bad about what he did to me? An eighteen-year-old schoolgirl who didn't know one end of a sophisticated Latin playboy from the other? Who was so naïve she thought that she'd found a fairytale romance to remember all her life?

Her mouth tightened into a twisted grimace. Oh, no, Vito never felt bad about me! Not for a second, an instant! Why should he? He simply twisted the truth into what suited him! Making *her* out to be the one to blame! That got him off with a shiny clear conscience…

The rage misted again in front of her eyes, and with a sudden jerking movement she hauled herself forward. Adrenalin was pounding through her. Rage and anger and fury and a burning compulsion that, whatever Vito Farneste might *dare* to throw at her head, she was not going to let him get away with it!

Her heels smacked on the wooden floor as she stalked across the room, yanking open the bathroom door.

The red mist of rage was still in front of her. Seven long years' worth of rage.

He was preparing to shave—razor on the vanity, hand reaching forward for his can of shaving gel. A white towel snaked around his hips, making his tanned Mediterranean skin look dark as bronze. The perfect musculature of his back, broad shoulders tapering to lean hips, was outlined in absolute detail. Each honed muscle and sinew and bone a paean to the human male form. He made her breath catch.

For a second she just stared, then—worse—realised that he had paused, slowly lowering his hand, and that his eyes were meeting hers in the reflection of the mirror.

And something was missing from them.

Something that had been there ever since he had nonchalantly got out of bed in the Rome apartment and informed her mother that her precious daughter had been 'gagging for it…'

It was not there now. Now, as her eyes met his, in the reflection of the mirror.

Time hung in the air.

And suddenly, devastatingly, Rachel realised that the last time she had gazed into Vito Farneste's eyes like this had been when he was cradling her in his arms, her body still trembling from the heavenly, miraculous journey into womanhood he'd just taken her on, smiling down at her, gently smoothing her hair back from her head while she gazed up adoringly at him.

'Mia bella ragazza...my beautiful girl—my beautiful girl...'

She heard the words. Heard them through seven long years. Their soft, accented murmuring, their tender cadence. She felt the kisses he'd dropped on her forehead, and then on each eyelid, and then on her lips.

She'd been in heaven.

And now, for a second, that moment seemed to be here again—her eyes holding his, drawn to him, held by him.

For an instant something seemed to dissolve within her. Some hard, ugly knot. Some malign, invasive canker that had been with her so long it had become part of her.

Something she could never be free of.

That had taken over her life.

But in that second, that instant, for the first time in those long years, she could feel it begin to dissipate...

Then Vito turned to face her, and the moment was gone.

His eyes rested on her again, but this time they glinted with malice.

Beautiful and deadly. Like the fallen angel that he was.

That he had always been, whatever sweet words he'd once murmured to her.

Now she was seeing the truth of him. It had always been there, but she'd been too blind to see it.

'Come to share my shower? Well, you'll have to wait a few minutes while I finish shaving. Another time, of course, we can try it unshaven. What is that term Englishwomen like to use? Ah, yes, rough trade—that's it. Is that what you like, *cara mia*? Rough trade? You must tell me—tell me everything you like your lovers to do to you. I wouldn't want my stud services to be inferior to theirs! But don't worry—I'm sure I can be as…inventive…as they, and give you a really memorable honeymoon.'

The glitter in his eyes made her feel sick. Yet as he leant back against the edge of the basin, razor forgotten, towel pulled taut across those lean, powerful hips and thighs, all but outlining the swell of his manhood, she felt her stomach hollow out.

Felt her gaze dragged down to feast on the body displayed for her so indolently, yet so powerfully.

Above the level of the towel each flat, taut abdominal band glistened, smoothing up over his solar plexus to fan into the subtle contours of pectoral muscles that flared out to sculpt a torso that would have graced a Renaissance statue dedicated to human perfection.

Last night I touched that body, caressed it, covered it with my kisses, took him into me, melded my body to his, wanted him so much, so much…

Through her veins the treacherous, traitorous weakness started to flow—a yearning, a terrible wanting that shook her with its power.

A power to make her want the man who stood there—whatever he did, whatever he said to her.

A power that shamed her.

Like a douche of cold, icy water she forced herself to drag her eyes upwards, away from his body, making herself see instead not the sculpted line of his mouth, or the heart-stopping planes of his face, nor even the dark, long-lashed beauty of his eyes, but only the expression in them.

That dark, veiled glitter.

He spoke again, in a drawl that seemed to scrape her nerves like fingernails on a board.

'Well, what is it to be, *cara mia*, this bright Caribbean morning? A vigorous, shall we say, *uplifting* session in the shower? Or something a little more languorous in the spa bath?'

His eyes were like daggers, each one drawing blood.

Her blood.

The breath raked in her throat as she spoke. Her voice was thin. As thin as the blade of a knife.

'I'm going now—going back to England. And I don't give a stuff about whether that makes our marriage illegal or not. Because I've got from it all I ever wanted—this marriage certificate! But I won't leave this place until I've told you something. You've twisted what happened in Rome seven years ago—twisted it out of all recognition! And maybe in that vicious, warped mind of yours you actually believe your version! But it wasn't like that—and you know it! You *know* it! I never planned anything. Nothing! *Nothing* of what you've thrown at me!'

The glitter in his eyes had gone.

So had the pose of indolent sexuality.

It was a pose—even now! He didn't mean—feel—a word of what he'd just proposed! It was just to shame you...humiliate you. Just like last night was to shame you, humiliate you...mock you with your own pathetic weakness to him...

She forced the shaming, humiliating knowledge away from her. What did it matter now? She was going to leave—walk out and never, ever see Vito Farneste again. He would never mock her, shame her, humiliate her again, nor sicken her with his corrupting sexuality...

But before she went she would throw at him every last ounce of her scorn, her disgust—her anger—at what he had done to her when she was eighteen!

She drew another raking breath, to speak again, but he spoke first. Hurling the words at her.

'Never planned anything?' Black anger flashed in his eyes. 'You dare to stand there and tell me you never planned the entire thing? You lied to me from the very start. You knew who I was! *Por Dio*, I was introduced to you at that party by name, and you never even blinked! But you hid your own identity from me very carefully, didn't you? *Didn't you?* Never mentioning that you knew who I was! Lying to me with a false name! Rachel *Vaile*!'

She stared.

'That's…that's my name. It always has been.'

His mouth thinned.

'You're illegitimate! Your surname is the same as your mother's! Your *unmarried* mother's!'

Her face set. 'She gave me my father's surname. It was all she could do—she couldn't put him down as my father. He wouldn't agree to it. He just laughed in her face when she told him she was pregnant. He gave her nothing—not a ring, nor maintenance, nothing. So she gave me his name deliberately. It's on our marriage certificate, in case you hadn't noticed…'

He brushed her gritted explanation aside without consideration.

'But you still didn't think to mention who your mother was, did you? Not for two whole weeks! When we spent every day, *every day* with each other! You never once thought to mention who your mother was! The mother whom you carefully primed to turn up so conveniently that morning, to catch her darling daughter in bed with her protector's son! Hoping my father would crack his outraged paternal whip and make me marry you!'

Cold accusation raked at her, his eyes condemning her.

Condemning her as a scheming, manipulating little bitch, trying to trap him into marriage…plotting with her mother—another scheming, manipulating bitch…

She wanted to rage at him, to shout her anger. She heard her voice rising.

'It wasn't like that! It was you—*you* doing the manipulating! You knew who I was all along! You deliberately seduced me! Just to get at my mother! And you threw the same vile words at me then as you've just thrown at me now! I hated you then and I hate you now—and, God help me, I'll hate you till the day I die for what you did to me!'

His eyes darkened.

'Tell me something.'

His voice was almost conversational. It raised the hairs on the back of her neck.

'If you hated what you say I did to you seven years ago, why were you so eager to come back for more after you bolted from Rome when your scheme to get me to marry you failed? You knew by then I wasn't going to marry you—yet you plagued me for the next three months! Turning up at my London office whenever you found out I was in the UK. Trying to get me to speak to you on the phone wherever I was! Eager to get more of what I'd given you a taste for! So...' he looked at her with his blank, cold look '...how does that fit in with your version of events as Little Miss Innocent?'

His voice was flat.

Rachel opened her mouth. Then, as realisation dawned, she closed it again. She felt again—as if it were yesterday, not seven years ago—the desperation she had felt when she had abased herself to try and get in touch with him, accepting every rebuff, steeling herself time after time to contact Farneste Industriale, desperate to speak to Vito.

How can I tell him why I was so desperate? I can't! I just can't!

And suddenly, in a black, drowning wave, she realised it was hopeless—hopeless to try and attack him, defend herself. He would justify himself at every stage.

Well, what did she care? She had no more need of Vito. He could rot in hell now for all she cared! She had, as she had just thrown at him, got what she'd come for.

And more—much more besides. Another lesson from a master deceiver. Dear God, let this be the last! The very last.

She turned away. She could take no more. Defeat hunched her, crushed her.

Vito Farneste had been a curse on her life ever since she had first set eyes on him. He was like a fever in her blood—unhealthy. Corrupting.

She had spent years trying to get the infection out of her bloodstream—perhaps now, after this ugly debacle, she might finally succeed in wrenching him out of her system.

Slowly she walked towards the door to the corridor.

'Rachel!'

His voice cut through the deadness in her.

'Go to hell, Vito,' she answered thickly, and left the room.

But it was no good telling him to go to hell. She wouldn't get rid of him that way.

Hell was where she was...

CHAPTER EIGHT

HE LET her go. A blank, black anger filled him.

So Rachel Vaile claimed she was innocent! Innocent as a newborn lamb. That she'd never tried to trap him into marriage!

His mouth thinned. Easy to say—oh, very easy to say— seven years later! But that moment when Arlene Graham had walked in on them would stay in his memory for ever. An eternal action replay that ripped from him everything he'd thought he'd known about the girl he'd spent two weeks with.

Devoting himself to her.

Devoting himself because—

No, he would not go down that path. It was a path marked for fools, and suckers, and fall guys. Patsies.

Just as he'd been.

He could feel the hollowing out of his guts, just the way they'd been gouged out that morning seven years ago. The moment he'd realised he'd been taken for a royal fall guy by his father's mistress and her daughter who, between them, had set a honey trap to clip his wings with.

Dio, but he'd fallen for it! He'd been totally taken in by her! Led up the garden path and tipped headfirst into the trap she'd dug!

But he'd refused to be trapped. Had walked out of it, skin free.

Memory leapt again.

Waking from sleep, hearing that harpy shrieking, seeing Little Miss Innocent—*not!*—clutching the duvet to her, gasping in fake shock as Mamma screamed at her, at him, yelling blue murder at his having seduced her precious virginal daughter. And himself, registering the set-up in a fraction of a second and realising there was only one way out of it.

Turning the tables on the pair of them!

With iron control he'd got up out of the bed, not bothering to hide his nakedness, and then casually, oh, so casually, reached for his jeans.

He could remember exactly what he'd said.

'Seduced her?' he'd drawled. 'She was gagging for it…'

He'd thought for a moment that Arlene Graham was going to have an apoplexy. She'd shrieked even louder, all but drowned out the reaction that Rachel had given.

He frowned, looking back down the years to that imploding moment.

It had been such a quiet sound she'd made. Not a gasp, nor a moan, nor a cry.

But something—he frowned more deeply—something that had sounded like something breaking…

His face hardened again.

Her reaction had all been part of the plan she'd laid with her mother! That was all. Arlene's part to play Accusing Mother, Rachel's to play Innocence Lost. And his father, of course, had been supposed to play Stern-voiced Paterfamilias, ordering him, dastardly Libertine Son, to make good the lost honour of Betrayed Young Girl…

Well, Enrico had not been so gullible! He'd cut his mistress down to size, silencing her shrieks of mock hysterical outrage. As for himself, his father had taken him aside later on and told him bluntly that if he had the slightest idea of marrying Arlene's bastard daughter he could find himself another company to work for—and it had better be a well-paid job, because he'd be out of the running to inherit Farneste Industriale…

He hadn't needed telling, of course. Rachel Graham—

Vaile—whatever name she called herself to try and sound respectable—could whistle for a husband to be caught in her honey trap!

Not that it hadn't taken long enough to shake her off! *Christo*, but she'd tried hard to get him back! A non-stop three-month campaign to get in touch with him.

God alone knew what had finally persuaded her to give it up! She must have finally got the message that he didn't want to know.

Or maybe she'd met another man by then. Lined up a more likely sucker.

Not, of course, that she'd managed to get anyone to marry her…

Until now.

He paced across the room, yanking open the wardrobe doors to haul out some clothes to wear.

His mood was foul. What the hell was he doing here? He should never have let his ego get the better of him and agreed to her ludicrous proposal! What the hell did he care if Rachel wanted him in bed or not?

His hand stilled on the shirt he was about to take off its hanger. A stone seemed to be filling his lungs.

Once he had called her his beautiful girl, his *bella ragazza*, held her in his arms, felt her body tremble in his embrace. He had kissed her with a tender passion that he had never before bestowed on any woman.

Because Rachel Vaile was like no other woman he had ever known.

And he had realised it from the first moment. Something had happened to him that night that he had never had any expectation of. It had been just one more party—he went to a lot of parties—and he'd cast his eyes around, keeping one open for women he didn't want to come on to him and the other for women from whose number he might choose to select one to amuse him for the night—or perhaps longer, if the mood took him. A few weeks, even, maybe a month or two. Nothing more than that. They got ambitious otherwise, started fancying their chances to get him to the altar.

But that was a place he'd had no intention of going. The scars ran deep. He'd seen what his father had done to his mother, the effect it had had on her, her life a living misery. And, though he might not intend to follow his father's path, he had known without vanity that any woman he married would want to cling to him, and if he got tired of her then severing the matrimonial ties would be messy. And besides, by then children might have arrived, and he would put no child through what he had grown up with, being torn endlessly between two parents.

So women would remain what they had been since he had first reached adolescence and discovered the power that his combination of wealth and looks could have. He was spoilt, he knew. Spoilt for choice. Had learned quickly that few women, if any, were beyond his reach if he so wanted. Married ones he'd stayed clear of. He'd seen enough adultery in his life, and didn't want to see more firsthand. He'd stuck to women who wanted what he wanted—an easy, sexually satisfying affair, with no strings, no meaningless hearts and flowers—had chosen women who could move in his world, stylish, fashionable, sophisticated.

A foolproof formula that had worked perfectly until that evening….

What had it been about her? The quiet English girl who had drawn his eye. He had never really been able to work out why. That air of being quite untouched, not just in the physical sense, which he could see instantly, but untouched by where she was. There had been two other English girls with her, both cut from quite different cloth. Sexually aware, sexually experienced. Assured and confident and quite at home. Wanting nothing more than to flirt, and dance, and sip their cocktails, and talk fashion and music and movies.

Rachel had been completely different.

He had spent two weeks—fourteen perfect, devoted days—finding out just how different.

She'd wanted to talk history. Art. Literature. Classics. Languages. Politics and economics.

But she'd been no bluestocking, trying to impress him. She had been just as happy throwing her coin in the Trevi Fountain, trying out every flavour of ice-cream, driving along the avenues of the Borghese Gardens in the pedal-powered chaises that could be hired there.

Happy gazing up at him with an adoration in her eyes that she hadn't even known was there.

But he had known it was there, and known he could not, must not, take advantage of it.

He must not lay a finger on her. She was a virgin. He had known that straight away, been able to tell she was utterly unversed in the ways of men. Did not even realise how powerful an allure that held.

For two long weeks he had held off. Using every ounce of self-control to stop himself from touching her, as he had increasingly ached to do. Knowing that if he did, then there would be no going back. Because her allure for him had grown with every passing day, every passing hour. His awareness of her had been intense—but he had not shown it. Had not let his gaze caress her silken hair, her clear, beautiful eyes, the tender curve of her mouth, the slender line of her graceful body, the delicate swell of her breasts, the sweet roundness of her bottom, the slim length of her gazelle-like legs…

It had become an ache. Wanting her.

And holding back from her.

Until that last night. She had been so melancholy beneath the laughing gaiety—she had relaxed in his company by then; he had drawn her out, made her feel safe, trusting him. The following day she would be returning to England.

It would be over. All over.

And suddenly he had known that it was not over. That it could never be over. That Rachel Vaile had become someone he would not, could not, let go of. Not when she sat gazing at him with such yearning in her eyes as they took their final coffee together in the Piazza Navona. The tourists there might not have existed. Only the girl sitting opposite had existed, with her gold silk hair and her wide, wanting, yearning eyes.

He had not been able to walk away from her.

And so, that night, he had done what he had wanted to do since the first moment he'd laid eyes on her. He had taken her, on an impulse that he'd known he should fight, but could not, would not, to the Farneste apartment, and in its baroque opulence he had cupped her face with his hands and lowered his mouth to hers. Finally doing what he had wanted to do since the first moment of seeing her.

And she had been everything and more that he could have dreamt of. Because he had never known a woman—a girl—like her. Had never before taken that beautiful, miraculous journey that made a girl a woman. He had been so careful with her, as if she were finest porcelain, and yet she had given herself to him with a sweetness, an ardency that had set his senses on fire.

And as he had lain with her, her tender body within the circle of his protective arms, he had known that something had happened to change his existence for ever. He hadn't been able to give it words, or a name, but he had known, as he cradled her silken head against him, his hand gently stroking her satin flank, their limbs tangled, their breath mingling, their hearts beating against each other's, in a closeness that had made him weak with wonder, that it was the most precious moment of his life.

Then, in the morning, the truth had arrived—in the form

of a screaming harpy—and he'd known that he had been taken for the biggest sucker in the world...

He ripped the shirt from its hanger and thrust his arms into the sleeves. His face was like iron. Hard and unforgiving.

But inside, somewhere in his guts, he could feel the same feeling that had ripped through him that morning seven years ago.

Searing, tearing pain.

By the time he left Ste Pierre Rachel was long gone. He didn't care. Not any longer. If there was any suspicion of false marriage he would trot out some tale of his over-emotional bride behaving like a diva just because he'd had to spend the morning catching up with his business affairs.

Which he did—taking a couple of hours on the phone and e-mail to Turin and London. Though he'd forcibly cleared his desk, to free up these days here in the Caribbean, the moment he got back in touch he was deluged. As he terminated yet another call, this time to his European head of ops, the memory of his father came to him again. Working like a demon and then calling time on everything, disappearing with Arlene. But even his mistress had not been able to de-stress him. Irritable, pressured, short-tempered—his father's moods had seldom been good.

A cynical curve pulled at his mouth. Arlene Graham had worked for her money, all right! Being his father's mistress had been no sinecure. She might have got rich pickings and an easy financial life, but his father could not have been easy to live with. She must have found it rewarding, though—she'd never decamped to another, easier protector. Maybe his father had doted on her more than he'd let on to his son.

A frown pulled at him.

But Enrico had left her nothing. Not even the villa. Unless

he'd been giving her cash on a regular basis, she hadn't walked off with any tangible assets from her protector.

Except the emeralds...

His mouth tightened. Well, he'd got those back now, and all it had cost him was a trip to the Caribbean! A bargain if ever there was one!

And, he added, his body forcibly reminding him, he'd got Rachel Vaile in his bed as a sweetener...

All she was good for now.

Whatever protestations she made, however much she tried to play that Little Miss Innocent card—dog-eared as it was by now—she was lying, he knew. If she'd been so innocent, so devastated all those years ago, as she'd tried to claim just now, then how come she'd been so keen to come back for more straight after? Plaguing him and pestering him and constantly trying to get in touch with him...

No, she was what he had discovered her to be that morning in the Farneste apartment, and that was all there was to her. She was a clever, manipulative, deceitful little operator.

And I still want her...

The stab of desire knifed through him, punishing in its urgency. He could feel his body surge, hungry for what it had had last night.

Because it had been good—better than good. Whatever Rachel Vaile had had at eighteen she still had—and more so! But this time around she could not play him for a sucker, because he had her number now.

And he wanted to dial it, right now.

Desire sucked at him. He wanted to feel her soft, silky body beneath his, wanted to see her hair fan out around her beautiful, impassioned face, wanted to feel again that satin sinking of his body into hers, feel the taut arching of her spine, the lush softness of her breasts thrusting against him, hear the soft, helpless moans she'd given as he'd stroked her higher and higher, into an orgasm that had convulsed her body, ignited his, rocking them both with its white-hot intensity.

What other woman could do that for him?

None that he could remember.

Rachel might be the one woman he would wish to perdition for what she had done to him in the past, but if she could do that in bed for him still then he wanted her still. Whatever the past had been, the present could be good for both of them. He couldn't present her to the world—let alone his mother!—as his wife, but he'd put her in a decent apartment in London, visit her discreetly.

Like a mistress.

With sudden decision he picked up the phone and ordered transport from the island back to Antillia. Then he called his pilot to get the jet ready.

There was one more phone call to make. Rachel had bolted, and, clutching that damned marriage certificate as she had been, there was only one place she was going. She was going to flaunt her marriage in her lover's face.

Well, she could do that if it humoured her—but it would be the last time she'd see that lover of hers until he, Vito, was done with her and let her have a divorce.

You married me, Rachel Farneste. You married me and I intend to enjoy my bride. So you can just dispose of loverboy, and I'll keep you satisfied instead.

She would be satisfied too—he would see to it. He would make her see that it was useless for her to try and convince him that what had happened seven years ago had been anything other than what he'd known it to be all along. And once that was out of the way he'd make her see that what they had now was worth putting their aggro aside for. So long as she didn't go on at him, trying to defend herself, he was prepared to keep her—for the sake of what she could do for him in bed.

He might even be prepared to buy her something to replace the emeralds with. Nothing as valuable, but something, he mused, that she could wear privately for him. Very privately.

His mind wandered off along enticing pathways, visualising her naked body glittering with diamonds...

He brought it back with a snap.

First he needed to see off lover-boy—and to do that he needed to find out who he was. Then he could get rid of him.

He punched the London office number on his mobile. The connection was fast and his call was answered instantly.

His voice was controlled. Very controlled.

'Mrs Walters? Get Security on the line, if you please.'

Rachel had dressed with great care. It was the same outfit she had worn to Vito Farneste's office. She didn't want to wear it, would have preferred to have burnt it on a bonfire as a warning to passers-by never to be as stupid as she had been—seven years ago or now. Stupid... Unbelievably so...

But she couldn't afford to squander any more money on another expensive outfit. Paying her airfare back from Antillia had eaten another punishing hole in her finances. Besides, the delicate lilac suit was exactly the sort of thing she would wear as Signora Vito Farneste. Exclusive, expensive, chic.

She travelled by tube to the Underground station nearest to her mother's hospital, but then, instead of walking the rest of the way as she usually did, she hailed a taxi. Signora Farneste would not walk. A taxi, at the very least, would be her mode of transport—unless it were a chauffeur-driven limo, of course.

Her mother wouldn't see the taxi, but the hospital reception staff would, and it would all add confirmation to what she was about to announce to her mother.

So would the ring glinting on her finger.

And most convincing of all were the precious marriage certificate in her handbag and the wedding photos she had collected from André as she left Honeymoon House. She'd forced herself to look at them, biting down hard on her lip as she'd done so. She wanted to put them on a pyre, with her outfit, but she needed them to show her mother.

Show how *happy* she was with her wonderful bride-groom, Vito Farneste…

The lie didn't matter. Only that it was sufficiently convincing to make her mother happy….

Her mother's happiness was all that mattered.

I don't matter. Vito doesn't matter.

We've got the rest of our lives ahead of us.

Her mother only had her life behind her…

Her sad, thwarted, unfulfilled life.

Grief clutched with its pincer claws.

But I can fulfil it for her. She'll know that she's leaving the world with her daughter fulfilling the dream she had for her…

She could wish all she liked that her mother had had a different dream for her—a dream that left Vito Farneste far behind in the disaster of her youth.

But you couldn't leave it behind, could you? You've let it haunt you, poison you, all your life since. Destroying all your chances to find happiness with another man. Just for the sake of a man like Vito!

They were nearly at the hospital. She took a deep breath.

Let Vito be behind me now. Let me finally be rid of him, free of him. Free of wanting him. Please—

Her prayer was pleading, urgent.

But even as the words formed in her mind her body gave a different message.

The memory of that night with him seared through her brain, and she bit down hard on her lip, trying to stifle it. Trying to douse the flame that had leapt in her blood.

It was as if she could feel the touch of his hand on her body, the feel of his mouth on her breast, the thrust of his body into hers…

Feel the urgency, the terrible, desperate urgency, of wanting him, wanting him, now, even now…

The taxi stopped. She jolted out of the memory.

Reality crushed back in, bringing the habitual heaviness of heart whenever she arrived at the hospital.

She paid off the driver and went inside.

'Good afternoon, Miss Vaile—you look very smart today!'

The receptionist—a familiar face by now—smiled brightly. Everyone was cheerful here. Relentlessly so. They had to be. Rachel understood.

'Do go on through,' the receptionist said, after Rachel had signed in.

Her mother was not sleeping. She was in a drowsy, sedated state, her mind clouded and confused. But her face lit as Rachel came in, and she reached out a weak hand to her.

Rachel's heart gave its customary painful squeeze as she looked at her dying mother and sat down, taking Arlene's frail hand in hers. She gave her mother time to accustom herself to her daughter's presence. Then, after a little while, she leant forward and carefully, tenderly, kissed her gaunt cheek. She took a breath, steadying her nerves.

This was it. No going back once she had said what she had come to say.

She smiled. Making the smile light her eyes, her face.

'I've got something to tell you—something wonderful…'

Vito straightened abruptly in his chair.

'She went *where*?'

'The McFarlane Clinic in Hampstead, Mr Farneste. She took the Northern Line Underground to—'

'Where is she now?' Vito interrupted the man from his

security agency with ruthless unconcern for the method Rachel had used to travel that afternoon.

'The subject returned to her home address at approximately six-thirty p.m. One of our operatives is watching the building, but the subject has remained within since returning there.'

Vito sat back again, his mind racing. A *hospital*?

What the hell was Rachel doing visiting a hospital?

'What kind of hospital is it?' he demanded.

'The McFarlane Clinic is a private general hospital. It—'

Once again Vito cut across him.

'Keep your man outside her flat. I'm on my way there. Phone me on my mobile number if she leaves the building.'

He cut the connection and stood up, tossing the phone down on the low coffee table.

What the hell was she doing at a hospital?

Was she ill?

The shaft of fear came from nowhere.

Illogical. Irrational. Incomprehensible.

He fought it—hard. He didn't want to feel anything for Rachel Vaile. Certainly not the irrational fear that had just sliced through him. *Maybe she was just visiting someone. Maybe she wasn't there for herself, but someone else.*

But who? Who meant so much to Rachel that she would go and visit them right after crossing the Atlantic?

Right after becoming Mrs Vito Farneste…?

His mouth set in a grim line.

Lover-boy. Was that who she'd gone to see?

Gone to taunt…

Taunt a man incarcerated in a hospital bed…

Grim-faced, he strode across the vast expanse of cream-coloured pure wool carpet and into the entrance hall. He punched the call button on the elevator.

It was time to visit his bride…

*   *   *

Rachel stared blankly at the screen of her laptop. She was supposed to be concentrating on translating the particularly tricky legal document that lay beside the computer. Her hefty Spanish dictionary was open on the table.

But she couldn't concentrate on her task.

Jet lag. That was what it must be. Crossing the Atlantic too quickly, too often. Even though she'd slept on the flight back from Miami, she still felt exhausted. Maybe it was just from being cramped sitting in an economy seat after the luxury of a private jet on the way out to Antillia.

Or maybe it was an exhaustion of the soul, not the body...

Her face was sombre.

I've done the right thing—I know I have.

Deliberately she recalled her mother's face as she had told her the 'something wonderful'. Through the pain and the confusion in her mother's face a light had lit.

'Oh, my darling.' Her mother's voice had quavered. 'Is it true? Is it really true?'

She had gazed, eyes blurring, perhaps, but fixed steadily, at the miraculous piece of paper that had achieved for her daughter what she had never been blessed with. Gazed at the photos of the fairytale wedding, her beautiful daughter in her gown with the Farneste emeralds around her neck— a true Farneste bride, with a true Farneste bridegroom beside her.

'Tell me!' she had begged Rachel hazily. 'Tell me everything!'

And Rachel had told her. Woven a fairytale romance that would have sat easily on the shelves of a library. A story in which Vito Farneste had met her again at a party, a party for the senior executives of a company she translated for, to celebrate a product launch. There'd been other VIPs there, she had told her mother, at a posh London hotel, and Vito had been one of them.

Eyes meeting across a crowded room, initial disbelief at each other's presence, and then—oh, miraculously—Vito begging forgiveness for how he had treated her all those years ago. He had been a callow youth. Rachel had told her mother that he'd said that to her.

He'd invited her out.

'I didn't want to say anything to you, Mum—I didn't want to upset you in case… Well, in case it didn't work out,' Rachel had said.

Then she'd smiled. 'But it did work out—that was the wonderful thing! And, Vito—well, he just swept me away! Literally! He took me to the Caribbean, and—oh, Mum—it was like something out of a film! He'd organised a special wedding on our very own honeymoon island and we were married Mum—*married*! Look!'

She'd held out her left hand and let her mother touch the ring circling her finger.

'Oh, my darling,' her mother had breathed again, and Rachel's heart had constricted to see the joy light her eyes.

Then it had constricted again, as her mother had gazed at her, her expression making Rachel want to weep, and said, 'I can die happy now.'

The knife in her heart stabbed again in recollection, and Rachel stared unseeing at her screen.

I did the right thing. I know I did…

She repeated it like a mantra. But even as she did she felt a hollow open up inside her. The hollow that had been there ever since she had left Antillia. A feeling of such emptiness that it could never be filled.

She had wrenched Vito Farneste from where he had haunted her for seven long poisoned years. Their vile, ugly confrontation had destroyed the ghost that had invaded her when she was eighteen, never to leave. But now she had this gaping, tearing emptiness inside her.

She would never see him again.

The knowledge should be nothing but relief, grim satisfaction. However badly she had behaved, forcing him to marry her as she had, his behaviour on the island had wiped out—brutally, devastatingly—any self-recrimination she might have been harbouring. He had destroyed completely any last frail vestige of hope that he might face up to what he'd done to her in the past.

She stared, grim-visaged, at the screen. *He thought you'd lied to him deliberately—not telling him who you were, luring him on to trap him...that you'd planned it all with your mother...*

Her jaw set. Luring him? Good God, she'd been an eighteen-year-old virgin still in the schoolroom! Just how alluring could that be, for heaven's sake? He'd been six years older than her, an experienced operator—oh, yes, very experienced!—who'd been helping himself to beautiful women since he was a teenager! Her mother had told her in that ghastly, horrible aftermath all about his reputation, his track record as a playboy, a lothario, a libertine...

No, she thought bitterly, accusing her as he had like that wouldn't wash! The boot had been totally on the other foot—though she'd been too stupid to see it at the time. All he'd done was try and twist his way out of it, put the blame on *her*!

Well, no way, Mr Drop-Dead Handsome Fallen Angel Farneste! You don't slime your way out of this that easily!

She let the anger roil within her, feeling its cleansing, coruscating power. Anger was what she wanted to feel, needed to feel. Anger at everything Vito Farneste had ever said, ever done.

Her jaw set even more tightly, tension pulling down the muscles of her neck until they ached, as she faced up to the final cause of her anger... He'd been able to take her to his bed again as easily as he had taken her that first trusting, gullible time.

Anger sliced through her. Deep and vicious. But not just at Vito. No, the biggest target was herself.

He deceived me twice—twice!

The old saying came to her: *Fool me once, shame on you. Fool me twice, shame on me.*

Well, shame on her, all right. Not just for her stupidity, criminal though it was, or for her folly in wishing, hoping, so stupidly that he had changed…but shame—deep, abiding shame—that she could not wash him out of her, that even knowing Vito Farneste for whom he was, a fallen angel, she could still desire him…

But I ran! When he said those things to me I ran! I didn't succumb to him! I didn't yield again!

And now he's gone. Gone from my life for ever. And I can be glad…at last I can be glad…

So why did the emptiness inside her feel as though it were eating her?

Rachel read the sentence again and frowned. No, it wasn't quite right. She reached for the dictionary. There had to be a more graceful way of expressing the point, which would be accurate, but not clumsy.

She was flicking the thin pages of the thick book when the Entryphone rang. She paused, tensing. The Entryphone buzzed again.

Memory of the last time she'd had a visitor here jumped immediately. Not even a week ago—but in that brief space of time she had been drowned in a maelstrom of tormented emotion.

The buzz came again.

It was probably just a charity collector, or someone getting the wrong flat. It couldn't be a social call. Since her mother's illness she'd cut out her social life completely—it was too painful, too unreal, to go out with former colleagues as she'd used to do when she was working. Some had tried to stay in touch, but she'd turned them away, unable to bear the normality of lives untouched by incipient death, unwilling to spend any free time she had from her freelance work apart from her mother.

While she still had her.

She spent as much time as she could with her mother. Just sitting with her in her room, sometimes reading to her, or chatting if her mother felt up to it. Sometimes attending to the precious little things that even the dying still clung to, such as brushing out her mother's hair, manicuring her nails. Sometimes she took her laptop with her and sat with it on her knees, working while her mother lay there, with the radio playing music softly.

Making up for all the years she hadn't spent with her mother when she was young.

She had wondered, when she had first conceived her desperate plan to achieve for herself the one thing that her mother had not, what on earth she would say to her about why her lifestyle had not altered a jot since marrying Vito Farneste. And then she'd realised it wouldn't be a problem. She had said as much that afternoon.

'I'll still come and see you just as much, Mum. Vito works a lot in London now—so we'll be living here. Oh, I'm sure there'll be trips to Rome, and Turin, but he knows I want to be here. With you...'

Her voice had trailed off.

'That's very good of him,' her mother had said, and there had been gratitude in her voice that had torn at Rachel. 'Not to keep you from me while...while I'm so ill. I...I know he won't want anything to do with me... I understand that.' Her eyes had dimmed a little, as if she was remembering painful things. 'He...he was always very close to his mother. It...it was hard for him. Seeing Enrico with me. It made *him* hard...'

Her words had faded, taking too much strength from her failing body.

The buzz at the door came again—louder and more insistent.

She was suddenly glad of the interruption, breaking off the chain of memory.

Pushing back her chair on the worn carpet, she crossed the bedsit to the door and picked up the phone. 'Who is it?' she asked.

The sound of Vito's voice at the other end made her clutch at the doorjamb. A bubble of hysteria beaded in her. What was that phrase? *It was like* déjà vu *all over again...*

And here was Vito Farneste, turning up on her doorstep again.

What for this time? Last time it had been to drop a bombshell in her lap.

What would it be this time?

'Open the door, Rachel.'

Vito's harsh voice demanded acquiescence. She let him have what he wanted—he would probably have his goons, or whatever, break the door down otherwise. She would end up being liable for the damage, and she could ill afford the expense right now.

She buzzed him in, taking the few brief moments while he climbed the stairs to her floor to try and steady her suddenly thumping heart.

Adrenalin surged.

The fear hormone. That was all it was. And with good reason. She knew that.

A sudden rush of panic that she was mad to let Vito anywhere near her again—let alone into her bedsit—almost overcame her. Then it was too late. There were footsteps outside the bedsit door and a peremptory rapping.

Slowly she opened the door to him.

As her eyes set on him she felt the adrenalin rush her body again.

Fear—it was just fear, that was all.

It was OK for it to be fear. Fear in respect of Vito Farneste was natural. Safe.

Any other cause of an adrenalin rush in his presence was not safe. Not safe at all.

Don't look at him!

But the adjuration was useless. Her eyes were sucked to him, unable to tear themselves away.

He was in a business suit. Dark, fine-tailored cloth, Italian in design, and so incredibly beautifully cut that he could have been parading it on a catwalk. But Vito wasn't the type to go flouncing down a runway.

Power radiated from him. Sheer, sheathed masculine power.

Her breath caught.

She fought for sanity, for safety.

'What do you want?' she demanded rudely, still pointedly holding the door open, even though he'd walked inside the bedsit. He'd cast a look around it disdainfully, the way he'd done the first time he'd marched in here.

He's probably never been anywhere this awful in his life, she thought bitterly. Well, she wasn't about to apologise for it. For anything.

His eyes swept back to her, lancing at her. Then he reached and took the door from her, shutting it urgently.

'Why did you visit the McFarlane Clinic this afternoon?' he demanded.

It was like a punch to her stomach.

'Wh—what?'

His eyes narrowed. 'You heard me. Why did you visit the McFarlane Clinic this afternoon?' he repeated.

Belatedly, she grabbed together what self-possession she could.

'That's no business of yours,' she gritted.

'Are you ill?'

She'd shaken her head before she could stop herself.

Something changed minutely in his face. But then, like a curtain coming down, an expression replaced it that chilled her to the core.

'Are you pregnant?'

CHAPTER NINE

THE question had come out of nowhere. It was something that up to this moment had not even crossed his mind. But the instant it flashed into his head he realised, with a hollowing sensation in his guts, that he might just have discovered that Rachel Vaile had been playing a much more skilful game than he'd allowed for.

Had he let himself be led up the garden path as to why she had really suddenly appeared out of the blue, eager to cash in on the Farneste emeralds at this particular moment?

Even though he'd safeguarded himself in the pre-nup from being ripped off by any future claims for child maintenance, even though he'd made damn sure he'd been protected up to the hilt on their wedding night, she might still have outmanoeuvred him. If she'd married him already pregnant...

Christo, was this what this farce was all about? Saddling him with another man's child—a child the natural father refused to marry her for? So she'd looked around for another rich sucker to be a golden meal ticket? OK, so he could always insist on a paternity test, and a negative result would see her off, but he'd bet his last euro she'd go to the tabloids with it and make as much fuss as she could, just to be vindictive.

He looked at her now, his expression icy.

She had gone as white as a sheet.

The kick to his guts was absolute.

So it was true...she was carrying another man's child.

Fury jackknifed through him.

But it was not, he recognised with disbelief, rage at Rachel.

It was rage at the man who had impregnated her.

Impregnated her and refused to marry her...

And rage at her too—for letting another man touch her. Like a light flashing on out of total darkness, momentarily blinding him, he felt a surge of raw, primitive possessiveness rake through him.

No man was going to touch Rachel again. No man was going to feel that lovely, exquisite body beneath him! No man was going to hear those gasping, aching moans coming from her throat as he caressed her. No man was going to hear that unearthly cry as her body caught fire with his...

Only him. Only he was going to have Rachel Vaile. Only him.

But he was too late. Another man had already marked her—possessed her—impregnated her.

Abandoned her.

She was staring at him, her face like chalk, and then before his eyes, slowly, with difficulty, she swallowed and the colour started to return.

'No.' Her voice was hoarse. 'No, I am not pregnant.'

She took a deep, shuddering breath that seemed to shake her whole, slender body. Her eyes slid away from his, unable to meet them, colour flaring suddenly in her cheeks before fading to a dull stain.

Relief surged through him. And then, hot on its heels, another emotion. So if she wasn't pregnant, if that wasn't the reason she'd gone to that clinic today, then what *was* the reason?

His original interpretation snapped back into his mind.

She'd swanned into the swish clinic dressed up to the nines—wearing exactly the same outfit she'd worn to confront *him*, Vito had seen immediately, from the surveillance photos his security firm had taken and e-mailed through to him on his way to this flat—and gone to brandish her precious marriage certificate in the face of lover-boy.

'So, I repeat, why did you go to the McFarlane Clinic this afternoon?'

His voice was implacable. He wanted answers—and Rachel Vaile would give them. Oh, yes, she would give them to him!

Rachel felt panic mounting in her breast. He'd had her followed! That was how he knew where she'd been. How *dared* he! But then he'd done it before—the last time he'd shown up here. Had her followed from his office all the way back from Chiswick.

But why have her followed now? The travesty of their wedding was over—she'd walked out. He should have no need to contact her again, see her again. Torment her again. Interrogate her again. Their divorce could be handled by his lawyers.

Her chin went up. Her movements were none of his business. Her *life* was none of his business.

'I don't have to answer that,' she replied. Her voice was composed—very composed. Not a tremor in it. She was proud of herself. But doubtful too—her voice might sound unwavering, but the adrenalin coursing round her body made her feel as weak as a reed.

And that question about her being pregnant had nearly cut her off at the knees…

Fear sliced through her. She could not be pregnant—surely to God she could not be! He'd used protection—she'd seen it. Had hardly paid attention to it at the time, but it had registered, all right.

Of *course* he had used protection! He'd made sure of it! God, the last thing Vito Farneste would want was to conceive a child by Rachel Vaile—the bastard daughter of his father's whore…

Pain iced through her, cutting through her flesh.

So much pain.

No—she would not go there again. *Must* not…

She must focus only on what Vito Farneste was doing now.

She needed defences. Urgently.

Anger would do.

She threw her head back.

'What the hell is this, anyway?' she demanded. 'Barging in here and asking questions that are none of your damn business!'

He ignored her protestation.

'You went to see your lover, didn't you? *Didn't you?* In that clinic! To flaunt your precious marriage certificate at him!'

Her mouth opened and then closed.

'Answer me!'

She gritted her teeth, steeling every limb. 'I don't have to answer you, Vito.'

Again he ignored her.

'What is his name?' he demanded. 'Your lover!'

He was insistent, relentless.

'I don't have to tell you!'

'What is his name?'

'I said it's none of your business!'

'Answer me!'

'I don't have to!'

Her voice had risen. His eyes were resting on her, as black as night. His voice, when he next spoke, was controlled.

'No, you don't have to. All you have to do is come with me to the clinic. As your *husband* I am sure the hospital will be happy to let me accompany you on your visit.'

Her face whitened again.

'No!'

'Yes.' His eyes never left hers, resting on her with a cold, dark implacability that made fear shake in her veins. 'In fact, as your husband, I'm sure the hospital would let me visit all on my own.'

Fear blazed in her eyes.

'No! You can't! You mustn't!'

'But I can,' he answered, his eyes pinning her down, skewering her. 'And I will.'

She made a convulsive gesture with her hand.

'No—please! *Please* don't!'

This was a nightmare. The idea of Vito Farneste turning up—getting into her mother's room...

She would have to phone the hospital at once! Tell them that if he turned up he had to be barred—banned! That he mustn't, *mustn't* be allowed anywhere near her mother!

Vito watched the fear play in her face and felt fury pound at him. Her desperation to stop him finding out who this precious lover-boy of hers was incensed him. She was *married*! To *him*! She had no business—no damn business!—going off to visit another man...another lover. Rage was consuming him. A hot, jealous rage that had taken him over, was driving him on...

He wrenched open the door.

'We'll go now—right now!' he said.

'No! I'm not going.'

'Then I'll go on my own!'

'I'll phone the hospital—tell them not to let you in!'

A humourless, wolfish smile iced across his face.

'You'll phone no one—I'll have my security man keep you company while I drive to Hampstead.'

She strained forward. There was desperation, hysteria in her voice. 'No! You can't! You can't go to the hospital! You can't see her! I won't allow it! I won't allow it!'

He stared at her, the door already yanked open.

She was saying something. Something that made no sense.

'I'll never let you see her—never!'

His brows snapped together. What was she talking about? Who was she talking about?

There had been hysteria in her voice. He'd have had to be deaf not to hear it.

'Who?' he demanded sharply.

Her eyes were bright—burning bright. Fevered.

Desperate…

'My mother!'

The words broke from her! She hadn't meant to let them out! Hadn't *ever* meant to let Vito Farneste know who she'd gone to visit. But if he did as he'd threatened—just turned up at the hospital, telling them he was her husband, and she wasn't able to warn them—they'd let him in. She knew they would! He was rich, powerful, persuasive…and he could probably get round any female receptionist in the world! She couldn't take the risk, she just couldn't!

So she'd had to tell him—

And now he knew. And because he knew he'd never go near the woman who'd been his mother's rival…

He was staring at her, and then, abruptly, he slammed the door shut and came towards her. She jerked backwards, bumping into the table, rocking her laptop so she had to grab it to stabilise it.

'Your mother? You told me she was abroad!' There was accusation in his voice. 'So what's she doing in hospital? Having a face-lift? Trying to stave off old age?'

The sneer finished her. Arlene would have no old age to stave off…

'No,' she breathed, her eyes fever-bright, the breath raking in her throat. Her hands clenched over the edge of the rickety table. 'She's got cancer.'

Her eyes blazed at him. She hated him, hated him so much. Hated the whole world, the universe.

She watched the blood ebb from his face.

'Cancer?'

There was something wrong with his voice.

His eyes had never left her, but she could see him mentally reeling.

'How—how long has she been...ill?'

Why did he ask? What did he care?

'Long enough. But don't worry, Vito—it won't last much longer. They want to move her out of the hospital into a hospice. Where she can—' Her throat was closing, but she had to say it. 'Where she can die.'

There was a brightness in her eyes, a burning. She blinked. But her vision didn't clear. Wouldn't clear...

She tried to speak again, but her throat had closed. Closed completely.

Through the blurring brightness in her eyes she saw him put out a hand to the door. Leaning against it. As if suddenly he could not support himself.

'Arlene is *dying*?'

She waited for the jibe. The scorn. The cruel, vicious quote about the wages of sin being death. Or the one about the mills of God grinding slowly, yet exceeding small...

But nothing came. Nothing except that look of total, absolute shock in his face, his eyes.

She blinked again. She could feel hot, painful tears squeezing into her eyes. She tried to brush them aside. She wouldn't, *wouldn't* weep for her mother in front of Vito— who loathed her, who had loathed her ever since his father had made her his mistress, his mother's rival.

She turned away, a clumsy, stumbling movement. She hunched forward, trying to stop the sobs rising in her throat, rising and rising like painful, agonising stones, forcing their way out of her body, her heart. She felt her knees weaken,

her legs, and she clutched at the edge of the table, sinking
down onto the chair that she'd been sitting on when the
buzzer had gone. She couldn't stand any more.

Her sobs racked her, harsh, tearing. Her head bowed, her
shoulders shaking.

Her grief was absolute.

Vito watched the racking of her body, the bowed head,
heard the tearing noise she was making.

He felt frozen. Immobile.

Then with a jerking movement he stepped towards her.
Haltingly, his hand pressed on her shoulder.

'Rachel—'

His voice was hardly audible.

He didn't know what to say, what to do. Shock was still
going through him—jolting, buckling waves of shock.

Arlene Graham was dying. The woman who had tormented his mother's existence until the day his father died.

And her daughter was breaking up over it.

Shock buckled him again.

There was something devastating about seeing Rachel
Vaile break down like that. As if she had become another
person before his eyes. Someone completely different.
Someone he didn't know how to react to.

Someone whose terrible, choking sobs tore at him.

He said her name again. He felt helpless. Useless.

She didn't stop crying. If anything her sobs intensified,
racking more powerfully through her body.

He felt his knees bend, and then he was hunkering down
beside her. Her hands were twisting in her lap, twisting and
twisting, writhing like snakes.

He reached out and took them in his, pressing them, stilling them.

She went on crying for what seemed a long, long time,

and Vito just went on kneeling beside her, his hands folding hers between his.

Gradually the sobs began to die away. She had no more left inside her. The convulsive shaking of her shoulders slowed, stilled. Slowly she raised her bowed head.

Her face was blotched, tear-stained, her eyes red-rimmed, cheeks runnelled with tears. Grief etched its unforgiving lines in every feature.

Her head moved towards him. In his hands hers seemed like cold dead weights.

'That's why I made you marry me,' she intoned, in a low, expressionless voice, her eyes blank as they looked at him. 'For her sake. To make her happy. She thinks—' Her voice choked. 'She thinks you've really married me—not just a piece of paper, but a real marriage. After all these years. That her daughter is a real Farneste bride. A fairytale bride and a fairytale ending for the end of her life.' Her voice changed, still low, but with a vehemence in it that scraped at him. 'And if you do *anything* to show her what a farce, a lie it is, then I'll kill you. I swear to God that I will kill you!'

She took a shuddering breath and went on, still with that same blank look in her eyes.

'At first I just wanted to fake the whole thing—pretend you'd married me! But I was frightened that she might ask to see the marriage certificate—just to convince herself it was really, really true—that what she'd always dreamt of had happened. I was terrified of what the effect on her might be if I couldn't produce one and she realised I'd been lying to her, feeding her a line, making the whole thing up. It would have destroyed her to have her hopes built up and then discover it was all fake. So that's why I had to make it real—real in the eyes of the law. So that I could look her in the eyes and swear that, yes, I was really, truly Signora Vito Farneste, show her the legal proof of it, swear to her

that it had been *you* who'd put the ring on my finger. Show
her the photos of me wearing the Farneste emeralds—a true
Farneste bride, just as she had always dreamt. That's why I
had to make it a real marriage—and the only way I could
think of getting you to do it was by offering you back the
emeralds.'

She paused, inhaling slowly, thinly.

'So that's what I did. And I don't regret it. Not for a
moment—an instant. I don't care what you do to me, what
you did to me. I don't care anything about you—you're not
important in any of this. And nor am I. Only my mother is.
And I don't care that you loathe and hate her, and it doesn't
matter that you loathe and hate me, and I don't care that I
loathe and hate you...I just care about my mother.'

Her eyes slipped away from him, down to the surface of
the table, down to her lap. Seeing his hands folded around
hers.

As if he were trying to comfort her.

With a sudden movement she jerked her hands away.
Then she pushed herself to her feet, scraping back her chair.
For a moment she just swayed, like a statue on an unsteady
base, and then she stilled.

She felt drained. Emptied out. Hollowed out. There was
nothing inside her. No feeling, no emotion—nothing. She
wondered why people said that crying was cathartic, that it
cleansed. She did not feel cleansed at all. Did not feel anything.

She rubbed at her eyes. They felt sore and swollen. She
turned and went to the kitchen alcove, splashed some water
on her face, using a tea towel to blot the excess. She wanted
a drink. A cup of tea. Something to settle her. She reached
for the battered kettle and started to fill it. She felt strange.
Very strange. And that was odd, because actually she wasn't
feeling anything at all. So how could she feel strange?

The water hissed into the kettle.

It was taken from her. Placed on the draining board. A hand closed on her elbow and turned her away from the sink.

'Rachel—'

It was Vito. She blinked. She ought to feel something about him, surely. Loathing. Longing. They were the usual emotions that she felt about him. But right now she wasn't feeling any of them. She wondered why.

She also wondered why he was leading her slowly but inexorably towards the sagging sofa that at night opened up into a lumpy bed. He sat her down on it, sat down as well.

'We need to talk,' he said.

He could still feel the aftershocks rippling through him. For the moment he put to one side his reaction to hearing that Arlene Graham was dying. He would deal with that later. Right now he was only trying to deal with Rachel.

She'd gone beyond shock, he could see. Retreated to some kind of numbed existence where nothing got through. He'd felt like that the day his father had died, succumbing to a second massive heart attack in forty-eight hours. It was a coping mechanism, he knew, that numbness. For himself, he'd used it to perform various necessary tasks.

Such as throwing Arlene Graham out of her villa.

As if he were disposing of the garbage.

Or tearing out a pernicious, parasitic weed that had been allowed to thrive too long.

When he realised that she'd purloined the Farneste emeralds as her pay-off it had been too late to stop her, and all his efforts to get the law to make her hand them back had failed uselessly.

But he'd got them back now. They were safe in the vault at his UK headquarters, and he'd be couriering them back to Italy as soon as he could.

His mother would want to see them again.

Even if they were nothing but a mockery to her. Mocking the bride she had once been—a Farneste bride, resplendent in the heirloom emeralds. But, alas, married to a man who one day would allow his mistress access to those emeralds...

A mistress who was now dying.

Whose daughter had used the Farneste emeralds to get him to marry her. Not to taunt a mythical lover who had declined to make an honest woman of her, but to weave a fantasy over Arlene Graham's final days.

A fantasy to vindicate her defeat seven years ago, when she'd tried to trap him into marrying her daughter—to make her daughter a Farneste bride worthy of the Farneste emeralds.

Round and round the convolutions went. Where did they start? Where did they end? Cause and effect, effect and cause, through two generations. Father and son. Mother and daughter.

He looked sideways at the daughter now. She was sitting very still, her knees drawn together, her forearms resting on her thighs, hands clasped together. Looking ahead of her at the dreary room.

He frowned. Why was she here, anyway, in this dump? Arlene was in an expensive private clinic, so there was money, all right—whatever she'd managed to hoard from her days as his father's mistress.

He heard himself voice the question aloud, and then wondered why. It was not what he'd intended when he'd told her they had to talk. Rachel's living accommodation was not top of his list right now.

She answered him without emotion.

'I sold my flat to keep Mum in the clinic. I wanted to be absolutely sure there'd be enough money to...to see her through it all. There isn't much left of her own money. And I knew I could never sell the emeralds—not even to you—

although I've been granted power of attorney over her affairs. I was going to give them back to…to your mother. They belong to her—my mother had no right to them. I know why she took them, but they were never hers.'

A shaky breath exhaled from her.

'But in the end—' She took another breath, a brief inhalation. 'In the end I had to use them. They were, as you told me so clearly when I came to see you in your office, my only asset.'

She turned her flat, expressionless gaze on him.

'I'm sorry I made you marry me to get them, Vito. It was the only way I could make my mother's dying wish come true. So I had to do it. But you've got them back now, and you can return them to your mother and divorce me and it will be as if this all never happened. Everything is over. The end. *Finito*.'

She watched him get to his feet. Felt something start to run inside her. An emotion, that was what it was— very thin, very fine, but an emotion, running through the strange, blank deadness that was filling her brain. She wondered what the emotion was.

He reached down and cupped her elbow, drew her up.

'Get your things,' he said quietly. 'We're going.'

She looked at him uncomprehendingly. Sudden fear flared.

'I'm not going to the clinic! You're not seeing my mother! I won't allow it! I—'

He cut across her. 'We're going to my apartment.'

She stared.

'I want out of this dump,' he said. 'And we still need to talk. But not here.'

CHAPTER TEN

SHE went with him docilely. She didn't know why she did. There was no reason to. But she did it all the same. She let him take her downstairs, out to the car—a swish silver-grey saloon—parked at the kerb. He opened the door at the passenger seat and she got in meekly, feeling nothing. He drove through the traffic, westwards across London, through Chiswick and out the other side to the business park, and drew up outside the Farneste Industriale building. He didn't speak, only concentrated on the driving.

She sat beside him, hands in her lap, the memory of his driving her around Rome in his fabulous car etched in her mind.

She did not look at him, only stared ahead, eyes bleak, unseeing.

It was strange to go back inside the Farneste building, so very strange. The faint mist of water from the fountains brushed her face, and she felt time revolve very slowly.

At this hour of the evening the place was almost deserted. Vito simply nodded at the security guard on Reception and crossed to his private lift on the far side of the lobby. It glided upwards, silently and swiftly. Again Rachel felt time shift.

But this time the bronzed doors did not open on the executive office level that Mrs Waters had taken her to. This time she stepped out into what was clearly a private hallway.

'In here.'

She walked in, silently looking around.

The flat was luxurious, with a pearl-grey carpet soft underfoot and an array of sofas in a slightly darker shade of grey.

'Would you like to freshen up?'

There was nothing in his voice beyond polite neutrality.

But that in itself was strange enough.

She nodded. Vito showed her to a guest bathroom off the hallway and left her to it. It was as luxurious as the lounge—white marble with stark black fittings. She looked at her reflection. Her eyes were still smeared and bloodshot; her face was drawn. She filled the basin with water and washed with soap, then took a moment to moisturise her skin with the travel kit from her handbag.

What am I doing here? Why did I come?

The questions went round in her head and she had no answers.

She emerged from the bathroom and went back into the lounge.

Vito was there, standing by an opened drinks cabinet. He was pouring out a glass of white wine. He held it out to her.

'Drink it. You need it.'

She took it in nerveless fingers and sat down on one of the huge sofas.

'I've ordered dinner. You need to eat.'

Vito's voice cut through years of memory.

She blinked, dragged back to the present.

'I'm not hungry,' she replied listlessly.

But when the food arrived, delivered almost immediately by a team of professional caterers, she found to her surprise that she was hungry after all. It was not difficult to eat the delicious, expensive food, beautifully presented in the vast dining room with its glass and chrome table and high-backed chairs.

They ate in silence, with the catering staff hovering attentively, always on hand to whisk empty plates away, refill glasses.

She was still feeling very strange, as if part of her had been cut away and was floating free in the atmosphere, bizarrely dissociated from the rest of her. She watched her knife and fork cut up the delicate folds of smoked salmon, followed by tender noisettes of lamb. She could see herself doing it, and yet it didn't seem to be her who was eating.

Her mind flowed along on its separate drifting track. She was not thinking, not feeling, just watching her hands cut up the food and fork it to her mouth, lower again and, at intervals, pause to reach for her glass—sometimes water, sometimes wine.

In the end she finished her meal and simply sat there, hands in her lap—waiting, as if she were a child, for her place to be cleared and to be told she could leave the table.

'Coffee in the lounge,' announced Vito, and Rachel wasn't sure if he was telling her or the caterers. But she slipped off her chair obediently and headed out of the dining room, sitting down docilely on the large grey sofa again. A tray of coffee appeared, its fragrance strong, with a silver dish of mints and tiny white chocolate truffles. She took one absently and bit into its tender surface.

'Cream?'

She looked at Vito, who had placed a large coffee cup in front of her and was now poised with a cream jug in his hand. He was watching her bite into the truffle and she wondered why. There was no expression on his face, but there was tension in his jaw, she noticed, and wondered about that too.

She shook her head. After so rich a meal she preferred her coffee black.

Vito put back the cream jug and picked up his own coffee. Then he crossed to the sofa she was sitting on and sat down at the far end. His weight depressed the soft cushions and she had to steady her saucer. A look of apprehension crossed her face.

She watched warily as Vito took a mouthful of coffee and then, almost with an air of decision about him, set it down on the coffee table.

'Why didn't you tell me about your mother's illness when you came to my office last week?'

She paused in lifting her coffee cup, staring incredulously at him.

She did not answer immediately. Did not know why he had asked a question to which the answer was so obvious it obviated the question in the first place.

'It was the last thing I wanted you to know!'

Her voice was vehement.

'So you let me think the worst of you instead,' he said tightly.

Her face tightened.

'I don't care what you think about me, Vito. You've thought the worst of me since the very first time you set eyes on me. Do you think I haven't forgotten the first words you ever said to me? You called me "the bastard daughter of my father's whore"! Not much of a glowing opinion, was it?'

Her voice was bleak.

A faint flush flared out along his cheekbones.

'I was angry that day. My mother had had another of her attacks, and yet my father had insisted on staying at the coast with...with Arlene. Nothing I could say would persuade him to go back to Turin.'

Rachel looked away. Her stomach had started to churn, and she didn't want it to. She wanted the numbness back. It was so much easier that way.

Vito was saying something else. What he said made her move her head around to him again, the same incredulous expression in her face.

'Was that why you agreed to plot with your mother to trap me into marrying you at eighteen? To get your own back on me for what I called you that day?'

His voice was taut and there was a guarded look in his eyes.

Here we go again, she thought wearily. Twisting the truth time again. Making Vito look squeaky clean time again. Making me out to be some manipulative slapper time again.

'We've had this conversation before, Vito, and it didn't get us anywhere,' she said tightly, the numbness creeping back over her. 'And there's nowhere for us to get to anyway. Just the divorce court, that's all—as fast and as painlessly as possible.'

A shuttered look came down over his face.

'I don't want to divorce you yet.'

The words fell into the air between them and Rachel just stared.

'What?'

His eyes were resting on her. Something was in them that quickened her flesh…

Suddenly she realised just how close, how very close, she was to Vito Farneste.

The numbness vanished.

'I…I don't understand,' she said faintly.

There was a look in his face she could not read.

'Don't you? Then let me show you.'

He leant forward slightly and took the coffee cup from her, setting it back on the table. In the same movement his hand slipped up around her neck, gliding smoothly over her skin. The churning in her stomach intensified.

His eyelids drooped. She had a second, maybe less, to realise his intent.

And then it was too late.

His mouth had lowered to hers, and like velvet on ice his

lips eased across hers, his tongue effortlessly opening her to him.

The blood surged in her veins, drowning her...

Drowning everything—her sense, her reason, her resistance.

She let him kiss her, let him taste her mouth, feast upon it, fingers working in the hair at the back of her head, his other hand closing around her spine, drawing her towards him. She felt arousal flare like a flame within her, hot and urgent and irresistible.

Everything vanished. Nothing existed except this—Vito kissing her.

Wanting her.

Desiring her.

And she wanted him too—wanted desperately the feel of his mouth on hers, his tongue twining with hers, his body pressing against hers, skin to skin, flesh to flesh, assuaging a hunger that would never die.

She heard her voice, deep in her throat, giving a low, helpless moan, and it seemed to inflame him. She felt him tilt her back—back against the sofa cushions—his hand easing down along her spine, cupping her hips, lifting the rounded swell of her bottom.

She could feel—shockingly, excitingly, arousingly—his hard, straining response to her, and she pressed against him more, another low, urgent moan escaping her. Her eyes were shut, tight shut, and all that existed was sensation...utter, blissful sensation, as Vito aroused her body for his possession.

His hand was lifting her top, sliding underneath, splaying out over the bare skin beneath, and then—bliss—curving, cupping around the aching swell of her breasts, sheathed in their bra, filling the fine material, straining against it. His fingers were cupping, stroking, and his palms were circling against the swollen, aching peaks of her nipples.

Oh, God, she wanted him so much! Ached for him.

No! Dear God, she must not let this happen!

She pushed him away. She could not, *could not* be so stupid yet again!

'No! Vito, please—*please* don't do this to me again! You *know* I lied to you! Telling you I didn't want you! I had to tell you that! I had to! I couldn't have borne it, forcing you to marry me as I did and then having you think I wanted you! You *know* I'm helpless over you! You don't have to prove it just to humiliate me again! I might have hated the words you used about me all those years ago—but I know, I've always known, that I couldn't deny it! The words might be ugly but it was true—dear God, it was true! I *was* gagging for it, for you, just like you said! I wanted you desperately! I made up dreams about you—stupid, childish dreams. Making you out to be Prince Charming, magically picking me out to be your Cinderella! Taking me round Rome like I was in the middle of some kind of fairytale!

'It was only when my mother held the truth up to me that I realised how incredibly stupid I'd been! If only I hadn't been so stupid I'd have seen what you were doing—I'd have realised that you were using me to hurt Arlene, and that I was playing right into your hands. She told me—she *told* me! Told me how stupid I'd been—thinking a man like you could ever be interested in a boring little English schoolgirl when you had an army of supermodels queuing up for you! They were the kind of women you were interested in—not an inexperienced virgin who didn't know one end of a man from another! I must have bored you stupid that night— even if I *was* gagging for it!'

He had gone completely and absolutely still.

Then, in a strange, emotionless voice, he said, 'Is that what Arlene told you?'

'Pathetic, isn't it?' she answered bitterly. 'That I had to have it pointed out to me? You'd been so convincing, you see, Vito. So wonderful, so beautiful, so gorgeous—and I really was very, very stupid at eighteen. I'm still stupid—totally stupid—weak and stupid—but at least now I know I am. At least now I realise you're just mocking me when you come on to me. Why do you think I told you I wanted a no-sex marriage?' she asked bleakly. 'I was trying, in my pathetic little way, to protect my pride—the pride you can shatter with one single touch! The way you did on Ste Pierre. Well, you know it now, so you can leave me alone. *Please* leave me alone...'

Her voice trailed off, everything drained from her.

He looked at her, his face closed, and then abruptly walked to the drinks cabinet, yanked it open. Rachel heard the chink of glass and then the glugging sound of liquid being poured. He turned and faced her, lowering his glass after having taken a slug of the whisky which gleamed like amber dew in the crystal tumbler.

'Do you know why I married you?'

The question came out of nowhere, and seemed to make no sense.

'Do you think it was to get the emeralds back?' he went on, his voice harsh. 'Do you? I'd have seen you in hell before I got them back on those terms! No one manipulates me—no one! I married you simply and solely to get you into bed. Because you'd stipulated a no-sex marriage! You stood there in your fancy outfit, looking cool as ice, and told me my stud services would not be required for the duration!'

She could feel her heart start to pound, slowly and heavily.

'So you took your revenge on our wedding night,' she said in a low voice.

He took another slug of whisky, then lowered the glass.

'No,' he said, and his voice sounded very strange to her suddenly. 'You did.'

She stared.

'I don't understand…'

He gave a sudden savage laugh. 'No, you don't, do you, Rachel? You don't seem to understand anything! And now I know why! Because your mother did such a number on you when you were eighteen.' He put his whisky glass down on the cabinet and started to walk towards her again.

'You've told me twice now that you didn't collude with your mother when you were in Rome with me. That the two of you didn't plan the whole thing together. I haven't believed you—I've refused to believe you. But now, finally, I think I do.'

He was still walking towards her, and her head flew up at his words.

'Well, that's big of you, Vito! That's really big of you! So you admit at last that you were a total bastard to me seven years ago! That you deliberately sought me out, knowing who I was at that party, and swept me off my feet. Remember, I was just a stupid, gullible, impressionable eighteen-year-old English schoolgirl virgin. I must have been a total pushover for you! And you deliberately, cold-bloodedly seduced me so you could hurt my mother!'

'No—no, I don't admit that.'

He was still walking towards her, with a long, steady pace, and suddenly, jerkily, she got to her feet. She backed away, edging around the low coffee table.

'You don't admit that it took a total bastard to tell my mother that I'd been gagging for it?'

'I thought I'd been set up. Trapped. I was angry.'

'Angry that she was daring to denounce you for what you'd done to me, you mean! Seducing me just to get at her!'

He shook his head, his relentless advance never slowing. She stumbled back and felt the closed doors of the lounge halt her retreat. She fumbled desperately with her fingers, feeling for the handles. She didn't want to turn her back on Vito—didn't dare…

'No. That's not why I seduced you.'

His voice was blank.

Her spine pressed into the door panels. He reached her, standing right in front of her. Blocking all escape.

Her heart was thumping like a sledgehammer, her breathing rapid.

He was too close. Far, far too close.

He put his hands out, one on either side of her head, caging her. She twisted her head to the side, panic-stricken, and then looked back at him.

He was looking at her. There was something in his eyes. Something that made her breath catch. Her legs weaken.

'You keep thinking,' he said, with that same strange, intent look in his dark, long-lashed eyes, the same tension along his high, sculpted cheekbones, the same tightness in his beautiful, sinful mouth, 'that there are only two possible explanations for what happened seven years ago in Rome. That either I set you up or you set me up. That one of us was the knave and one the fool.'

'Well, it wasn't me who set you up, Vito, so that only leaves you who set *me* up!'

'No—there's a third explanation. And it is the true one. I know that now.' He paused a moment, and his eyes were searching her face. 'One evening, seven years ago, I turned up at a party, having just disposed of a girlfriend who had started to bore me—as, after a while, all my girlfriends started to bore me. And while I was there I met someone who was like no one else I'd ever known. Someone who took my breath away! She was young—too young for me. And not my kind. Not my kind at all. I liked sophisticated women who were chic, and sexy, who flaunted their *bella figura* and knew they were desired and desirable. Who fell into my bed very easily and knew exactly what to do when they were there. And knew just when to get out when I got bored of them. But the girl I saw at that party that evening wasn't like that. Not at all.'

He paused, a strange expression coming into his eyes, as if he were seeing darkly down the corridors of time.

'She was a virgin. I could see it at once. The two friends that she was with were not—I could see that too. And I knew that because she was a virgin I really, really should leave her alone. But I couldn't. And I didn't want to. I wanted to go to her, talk to her, get her away from the party—which was no place for her. Get her to myself. But not to have sex with her. Though I longed to—how could I not? She had hair like spun gold and the clearest, most beautiful eyes I'd ever seen in a woman. She talked to me about Michelangelo, and the Renaissance, and Latin writers and Italian history. And all the time she talked she never tried to flirt—not once. She just looked at me with those clear, beautiful grey eyes, her hair like a shining waterfall and her face…ah, her face…like a Botticelli painting. After I'd driven her round Rome, shown her the city by night, I took her back to her apartment and said goodbye to her. Knowing I must not see her again.'

He drew breath, then kept going. 'But by the morning I knew I had to. So I went back to her apartment and took her out again. Every day. For two weeks. I showed her Rome and Ostia and the Lazio, spent every day with her. She soaked it up—every last bit of it. And every day, every hour, I was drawn to her more and more. I didn't dare touch her. I knew that if I did I would never let her go. But she made it hard for me—so hard. She was so beautiful, so lovely—so…pure. I don't mean just sexually, but… spiritually. She had an ardency about her, a passion, but it was not venal. It was a flame, burning in clear air, not an appetite to be sated. I was…enchanted…by her. I wanted to make her mine.

'And so the last night before she had to return to her real life, when the summer moon was riding high, its pale light giving her face yet more unearthly beauty, I knew that I could resist her no longer. She wanted me. I knew she wanted me. She tried to hide it, but she could not. It bewitched me even more that she should be so shy about it, so hesitant about her desire. But her hesitation dissolved in a second, an instant, when I kissed her, when I made love to her.

'She was so beautiful, so lovely—and she gave herself to me in all her beauty. There had never been a woman like her for me. And I knew there never would be again. She was mine. Safe in my arms. All through that long, blissful night.'

As he spoke, his words like a healing balm upon her, something loosened inside her. That tight, knotted lump, that hard, stony canker that had been inside her so long, for seven long years, began to dissolve.

'Do you mean it, Vito? Do you really mean that? That that was how it was for you?'

Her voice was a whisper. A plea.

'Yes—until the morning. Then all my illusions were ripped from me. And I realised that the beautiful, grey-eyed, silk-haired girl that I had made my own was nothing more than the willing tool of my father's mistress, who had used her for her own machinations.'

Rachel's eyes shadowed.

'She didn't. Oh, God, Vito I swear she didn't know I was there—she didn't even know I was in Rome! I never told her—I knew she would never have given me permission. She told me...afterwards...that she had always been fearful of you. That you might have thought it amusing to seduce me just for the hell of it, to get at her!'

She looked at him, a pained, wounded expression in her eyes.

'I know I should have told you who I was the moment I realised you didn't remember that I was Arlene's daughter—but I couldn't bear to! I knew you'd hate me, just like you hated my mother. You wouldn't have come near me—and I couldn't have borne that! It was so magical, so wonderful, when you took me up, spent your time with me! I couldn't spoil it all. I just couldn't!'

He looked at her sombrely.

'It's true—I would not have stayed with you had I known who you were. That's what made my anger that morning so great. Discovering I'd been played for a fool all along. That you were not the person I had built you up to be.'

He paused. 'But all along you were, and you are that person. You are that most beautiful girl, *mia bella ragazza*. The girl I held in my arms that night—never the other one. Never! And to know—to discover—' there was a crack in his voice as he spoke '—that my illusions were not illusions after all. That you were—*are*—the person I thought you first. Oh, dear God, you do not know how much that means to me! Rachel—' The crack in his voice came again, and his dark eyes were filled with an emotion that flowed from them, stopping the breath in her throat.

His hand curved around her cheek and she felt herself yearn to lean into it, to feel its strength supporting her. But she dared not. The canker inside her had grown for seven long years. It would not loosen its grip without a struggle.

'Rachel...' He said her name again softly, his gaze melting through her. '*Mia bella ragazza*—my beautiful girl...'

His kiss was like the first time his lips had ever touched hers. And in that sweet, exquisite moment she felt a tearing, a cracking, as though something hard and cruel and ugly were finally being cut from her body.

Releasing her from its consuming grip.

The tears slid from her eyes and her hands slowly, so

slowly, curved around him, to hold him, just hold him, as he kissed her.

He eased her from him.

'Come,' he said, and took her hand. She clung to it, going with him blindly, fatefully.

In the dimness of his bedroom he took her garments from her one by one, until her body glimmered in the night. He did not touch her until he was naked too, and then he led her to the bed and laid her down upon it, her hair like a veil across the pillows.

He leant over her and smoothed her hair.

'My beautiful girl,' he said, and softly kissed her mouth, her eyes, her breasts and all her body, until she was a single, pale burning flame.

'Vito...' she breathed, and his name was an invocation and a blessing, a healing and a benediction.

He lifted her arms above her head, one and then the other, holding her hands with his. He arched over her, bending to kiss her mouth with one last, soft kiss before his body slid into hers and found the union he sought.

She cried out, a high, keening cry, and for a moment he hesitated. Then she strained her hips to his.

She cried out again, this time his name, the pale flame flaring.

Setting fire to him.

He lifted his head, bearing down upon her raised hands, his spine arching back, and when the final thrust of his body took her the burning flame sheeted through her body like a flash fire. And as her body burned in its intensity she saw that he was burning too, his body incandescent.

She drew him down to her, folding her arms around him, feeling the smoothness of his skin beneath her fingers, caressing him until he lay still and quiet in her arms.

At peace again.

His voice was shaken when he spoke.

'I should have trusted you—trusted myself. The body does not lie—it cannot! What we had that night was the truth! Everything that came after was the lie.' He looked into her face, his eyes pained. 'And if you hadn't come to me, to offer me back the emeralds, the lie would have lasted all our lives. Its poison festering still.'

His expression changed suddenly.

'Why did you try so hard to get in touch with me after you'd gone back to England? After what I'd said to you, what you thought I'd done to you?

The question had come out of nowhere, and she felt herself tense in his arms.

He looked across at her, a troubled look in his eyes.

'Seven years ago you tried to get in touch with me and I wouldn't let you. Why? Why did you do so? I'd rejected you so totally. Were you trying to convince me that you had no part in what I'd accused you of? Yet why should you plead your case to me if you thought me the one who was guilty?'

As he spoke he saw the apprehension in her eyes. The reluctance to answer his question. From nowhere, a sliver of doubt began to worm into his mind.

'It's so long ago, Vito—it doesn't matter now. Truly it doesn't.'

The worm eased forward, insinuating itself into his consciousness. He found his breath quickening.

'But tell me all the same. God, Rachel—day after day you phoned, and I would never talk to you! Even when you managed to get through to me I hung up on you! Why did you keep phoning? It torments me that you were so close and I turned you away! We might have made our peace if you'd convinced me of your innocence! Was that what you were trying to do?'

Her eyes clouded. Had she pulled back from him slightly?

He did not know. But a coldness was seeping through him. She was hiding something...

Hiding something just when he'd thought that all the poison had been drawn, that the way between them was clear and clean.

'Tell me!' There was an edge in his voice.

Her face tightened, and this time she did draw away from him, straining back against the circle of his arms. Instinctively he tightened his hold on her.

'Tell me!'

For one second longer she hesitated, that look of apprehension in her eyes deepening.

'I...I wanted to borrow money from you, Vito.'

The words fell from her mouth and he could not believe them.

'What?'

She flinched. 'I needed money. I...had to...to disappear. I couldn't go to my mother for money, and I had none of my own. So...so I went to you, because you were rich...'

He stared at her, disbelief in his face. 'After what I'd said about you, you thought I would lend you money?'

She seemed to flinch again, and though it hurt him he could feel the anger begin to well up in him—anger and doubt, seeping their poison through him.

'I...I thought it would be in your interest.' Her voice was flat.

'Why?' His voice was hard.

'Please! Please don't ask me, Vito! It's a long time ago. It's over!'

She strained away from him again. But his hands pressed against her back, holding her.

'Tell me!'

Something shifted in her eyes—something that made the worm writhe in his mind.

'Have I been wrong about you after all?' he demanded. 'Have you been making a fool out of me even now? Tell me!'

She told him.

'I was pregnant. I thought you would be willing to lend me enough money to disappear—just to tide me over until I could get settled and claim benefit...or...or get a job... Anyway, be independent financially, able to bring my baby up on my own. I thought that it would be in your interest to help me because if my mother had discovered I was pregnant she'd have...she'd have made such a fuss, and it would all have started up again...her trying to make you marry me when you didn't want to... I thought you would be willing to lend me money to get rid of me, make sure she never found out. But...but in the end it didn't matter. I miscarried at thirteen weeks, so I didn't need any money after all. And I got a job, and started night school instead...'

Cold ran through him. Icy, freezing water that deluged through his body.

She was talking again, and as he heard her words the icy, freezing water deluged through again.

'I'm sorry! I'm sorry, Vito! I should never have told you! I knew you'd be angry—discovering that I came to you to get money. I knew you'd think I was trying to blackmail you, trying to get a pay-off from you! But I swear I wasn't— I swear! I just needed enough to...to tide me over. So I could disappear.'

Disappear...

The word tolled in him.

His arms around her went slack.

She pulled away from him, getting out of bed. She seemed to be stumbling, finding it difficult, her movements jerky, uncontrolled.

Pregnant. She'd been pregnant.

She'd been pregnant—and broke—and desperate.

Desperate enough to force herself to keep trying to get in

touch with him, day after day, accepting every rebuff, every
curt, cold refusal to talk to her...

*I turned her away. She was carrying my child and I
turned her away...*

Guilt so great that he thought it must kill him pierced him
to the core.

He thought of the rage he had felt only a few hours ago,
when he'd thought that a man might have impregnated her
and walked away.

*I was that man. It was me—I did it to her. And I turned
her away when she came to me...*

For one long, endless, horror-filled moment he watched
her reaching for her clothes, trying to pull them on with
those jerky, uncontrolled movements.

Then in a single bound he was there, clutching her,
clutching her with a desperation that filled his soul.

'I'm sorry—dear God, I am so sorry...' The words
choked from him, painful and agonising. 'I thought I had
cause to hate you. But you... *Christo!* You have cause to
hate me a hundredfold! And what burns me even more than
knowing that I turned you away—turned you away when
you were carrying my child—what burns me even more
with shame is that you were not even hoping for anything
more than that I would be glad—*glad* to get rid of you!
Glad to give you the money to disappear...'

His voice dropped. His head bowed.

'And you lost our child. Our child died. If you had had
care, physical and emotional, it might not have happened—
if you had been with me, if I had been looking after you...it
might not have happened.'

His hold crushed her.

'I'm sorry—so sorry.'

She was crying, the tears pouring from her silently, ceaselessly. He held her in his arms, cradling her and rocking
her, slowly, gently, while the tears flowed.

And in his own eyes the welling moisture stung like acid.

He carried her back to bed, carried her in strong arms that would never let her go again, and held her against him while she wept for what had been lost.

When she was still, when all the pain for their child's brief, doomed existence had ebbed, he spoke.

'So much has been wasted, and this is the most final waste of all. But we have been given a new chance, and I beg you—I beg you, my dearest love—that this time we will keep faith with each other. Stay with me, and be with me, and I with you. *Ti amo*—I love you—and with all my being I pray that you can love me as I love you.'

Rachel heard the words, but she could not believe them. Emotion was still pouring through her—at last the grief she had felt for the loss of her baby, so long ago, at last, the acknowledging of the pain of that loss. So much emotion was overwhelming her, and through the pain and grief came something so wonderful that she could not believe it.

Dared not believe it.

Vito had never set out to debauch her, to use her to wound her mother. Never! What had happened that magical fortnight in Rome had been between them only—her and him—as if there were no Arlene, no Enrico, no tormented, tortuous convolutions of infidelity, adultery, torn loyalties...

What we had was real—real and true and ours, just ours...

And now they had it back.

After seven long, bitter, cruel years of hating and despising, loathing and misjudging, they had it back.

And they would never let it go again.

Never.

Ti amo...I love you...

Had he really said that? Had Vito Farneste, the most beautiful man in the world, really said that to her?

She felt a glow in her—a glow that would keep her warm, she knew, for the rest of her life. The warmth of being loved, so wondrously, so miraculously, by the man that she loved…

At last I can say it—at last I can say what I have felt for him ever since that time in Rome, when I fell in love with him and gave myself to him. I tried to tell myself afterwards that it was nothing more than a stupid schoolgirl infatuation, and then, later, nothing more than lust, desire, wanting.

But it was love.

Love all along…

Happiness filled her, so deep, so profound that it overwhelmed her, pouring through her like a rich, costly blessing. A blessing on them both.

We have found each other again, and we can never lose each other now…never again…

And then, into her happiness, her wonder, came a dull draining of her joy.

How could happiness be theirs?

The past stood between them. Not their past, but their parents'.

A sob half broke from her, and she stifled it.

'Oh, God, Vito—it's all no use! No use! We can't love each other—we can't!'

He lifted from her, his eyes filled with concern.

'How can we be together? How? My mother was your father's mistress—your father betrayed your mother to commit adultery with mine!'

Vito's face tightened.

'The past has spread enough poison into our lives, *mi amore*—they made their choices, each of them. Your mother to be my father's mistress. My father to commit adultery. My mother to stay with him when she could have left him because of his betrayal. They made their choices and we—' he took

a deep, sharp inhalation of breath '—we must make ours.'
He looked at her, deep into her eyes. 'I choose you, my
most beautiful girl, my dearest one, my beloved. I choose
you. To be my love, to be my heart, to be my wife and my
soul, for all our days.'

His mouth lowered to hers, and with a kiss he sealed his
promise, his choice.

EPILOGUE

'VITO, you don't have to do this—truly you don't.'

Rachel's voice was diffident as she paused outside the door in the quiet carpeted corridor.

He took her hand. 'Do you think so ill of me that I would begrudge a dying woman her final peace?'

She shook her head. 'Her death changes none of the cause you had to hate her.'

He gave a low sigh.

'It was not my place to hate her. I hated her because of the pain she caused my mother.' His voice dropped. 'I know she might have been the mistress, but the adultery was my father's. And, for all my calling her predatory and greedy, my father was never one to be taken advantage of. The greater fault was his, not hers. It was just more…convenient…to make her the villainess. My father was a difficult man—your mother earned her place with him. So—' he squeezed her hand '—please don't be afraid that I will say anything now to upset her.'

Her throat was tight as she answered, and her voice husked.

'Thank you. She has so little time left.'

He lifted her hand and pressed his lips to it. 'Then let us show her that her final dream for us has come true.'

He turned the handle of the door and led her inside her mother's room.

As his gaze rested on the figure lying in the bed his first thought was that he surely could not be in the right room. Could the gaunt, stricken woman with greying hair lying there be the woman who had tormented his adolescence?

His father's expensively dressed mistress, with her immaculate maquillage and perfect hair and varnished nails? Had Arlene Graham come to this?

As he halted Rachel was walking forward, up to the bed.

'Mum?' she said softly. There was something in her voice that made Vito's throat tighten.

The woman in the bed stirred slightly, her head moving on the pillow so that she was looking towards the source of the voice. Her eyes focused and Vito, with another jolt to his system, realised it was an effort for her.

'Rachel—my darling.' Arlene's voice was faint, but Vito could hear the joy in it.

Then the gaze shifted slightly, moving from Rachel to him.

And something quite extraordinary happened.

The gaunt face lit, as though the sun were shining through her eyes.

'Enrico—is it you? Is it really you?'

A frail, veined hand lifted from the bedclothes, then fell back.

At his side, Vito could feel Rachel stiffen. He took a step forward, coming up to the bed. Pale eyes searched his face with an expression in their depths that he would have been blind not to recognise.

Dear God, Arlene Graham had loved his father. Only love could light her stricken face like that, just for a moment making the illness vanish from her features, just for a brief moment making beauty reappear.

'Enrico…'

The faint, beseeching voice came again.

He reached out his hand, pressing it down over her frail fingers.

'*Si.* I'm here, *mi amore.*'

How could he deny her that at such a time?

For a moment something flickered in her eyes, and with

a sense of dread in his heart Vito realised what it was. It was hope.

Then it faded, and into her eyes came a shadowed look. 'No,' she said softly. 'Not Enrico. I was never his love.'

The faded eyes searched Vito's face, and then a new wonder came into them.

'Vito.' His name was a slow exhalation. Her eyes moved slowly towards her daughter, standing back a little, her expression full. 'Rachel—then it is really true?'

Vito turned and drew her forward. He could see the tears spilling in her eyes and his throat tightened even more.

'Yes, it's true.' He spoke quietly to the woman lying there at the end of her life. 'Your daughter is my bride. My wife. And she is more than that—so much more. She is the woman I love—have always loved, will always love. And I ask—' his voice thickened '—I ask your blessing on us.' He paused, hardly able to go on. 'For the sake of your love for my father, which I never... I never knew.'

The frail fingers pressed his briefly, with no strength, then slipped from his grasp. But it was with more vigour that she spoke, as if surfacing from some other place where she now almost always dwelt.

'He did not want me to love him. But I did all the same. Just as your mother loved—' Arlene's voice stopped. A sad, bitter smile haunted her mouth. 'We had more in common than we wanted. Each loving a man who did not love us...could not love us. Poor Sylvia. At least I could be with Enrico openly—your mother did not even have that. All those nervous attacks she had to endure. They gave her the reason she needed to flee to her chalet in the mountains, where he could come to her...'

The blood was running cold in Vito's veins.

'Who?' The question breathed from him.

Arlene's misted eyes looked at him. 'She never told you? No—she would not. She has protected him always. The scandal would be terrible. Even now, as a widow. As Enrico's wife—she would have been destroyed.'

Disbelief was emptying through him.

'*Who?*'

The urgency in his voice reverberated in the room. Beside him, Rachel was standing motionless.

Her mother looked at Vito with clouded eyes.

'You called him Tio Pietro—'

Vito's expression froze. '*Por Dio—*'

Tio Pietro—an old family friend. And a cardinal of the church.

'There was never an affair. Your mother never even had that. Only an emotional friendship that could never be more because of his vows. Poor Sylvia...'

Arlene's voice weakened, her eyelids closing as she succumbed once more to the drug-induced sleep that shielded her from pain.

Vito stared sightlessly. The world he had grown up in had dissolved beneath his feet. All these years of seeing his mother as a victim. And all along...

He turned away, hunching, hands fisting at his side.

Arms came around him. Folding him to her. She pressed her cheek against his back. The only support in a world which had just been rocked to its core. Rachel said nothing, only let the bitterness buckle through him. Then, at last, she spoke.

'Vito—it was their lives. We cannot judge them. We must not. We must only—' her voice cracked as she spoke '—only be glad that their lives are not ours. That we have been given a chance—a choice—for happiness, love, that they did not have. Was your father capable of loving a woman? Certainly not my mother, though she loved him. And your mother—doomed to love a man who could never love her as a woman. We cannot judge them—we can only pity them. And be glad, so very, very glad, that our path is different from theirs.'

Her arms turned him around and her hands slid to cup his face, her eyes gazing imploringly into his blank, wounded eyes.

'We have so *much* compared to them.'

A long, deep shudder went through him, and then, as something passed from his face, he reached to take her hands and hold them in his.

'You're wrong,' he said, and at the moment when he saw the pain lance through her eyes at his words he bent to kiss her. Sweetly, tenderly, lovingly and eternally. He lifted his mouth from hers. 'We have everything. Because we have each other.'

And he lowered his mouth to hers again.

Thin sunlight filtered through the branches of the trees, bare still, yet with the green flush of spring returning. Life returning.

But Rachel's eyes were only on the gaping darkness of the earth as her mother's coffin was slowly lowered into its final resting place. Tears slid ceaselessly down her cheeks.

'Earth to earth, ashes to ashes, dust to dust; in sure and certain hope of the Resurrection...'

The priest's sonorous tones rose and fell. At Rachel's side the tall, somber figure of her husband stood by her, head bowed. And on her other side stood another figure, shorter than her, very elegantly dressed in black, her graying head also bowed.

The committal ended, the priest came over, taking her hands, murmuring words of kindness and comfort. Then, with a brief word from Vito, he nodded gravely and walked a little way away. Rachel took a step forward. Into the grave she let fall the posy she had been clutching in her hands. Tiny pink and white rosebuds, as delicate as a baby's breath.

Then she stepped back, and Vito was there to fold her to him.

'My dear child.'

Another voice spoke. Italian-accented, soft and low, veined with sorrow. Rachel lifted her head and turned, blinking tears from her eyes.

The other woman kissed her gently on each cheek.

'Your tears must only be for yourself—not for your mother. Grieve for your loss, but do not grieve for her.' The woman reached out a hand and gestured to the gaping grave, and to the other grave beside it, with its marble headstone and iron railings all about. 'She is with him at last,' she said quietly. 'Nothing can separate her from him now.'

Rachel swallowed painfully. 'It's so very good of you—' she began in a low voice, but the other woman interrupted.

'No! It is her place. It was never mine—never. I should never have married Enrico—I knew I did not love him. I knew my heart would for ever be Pietro's—even though he did not want it—even though his vocation called him to the priesthood. But your mother loved Enrico, and her place in death is at his side. And your place...' she paused, and Rachel could hear the break in her voice '...is with my son.'

She paused again, emotion filling her face, taking Vito's hand and Rachel's together as they stood in the quiet cemetery where Arlene Graham now lay beside Enrico Farneste.

His widow's dark eyes rested on her son, and on her daughter-in-law.

'Out of all this pain, all this sorrow, time has healed us all. And you have been the healing. Your love for each other has made recompense for the past—the past that belonged to me and Enrico, and Arlene and my Pietro. We caused you pain, both of you, yet your love for each other is my comfort and my consolation.'

She smiled then, a sad, sorrowful smile, but it had acceptance in it. And benediction.

'And now there is a new generation—a new blessing. Your mother died in the knowledge, my dear child, that the grandchild for whose sake you placed that posy in her grave will shortly take its place in the world. And it will have the greatest blessing a child can have—parents who love each other, who stand by each other, loyal and true. *Your* parents could not give you that blessing—and much grief came of it for you—but *you* can give that blessing to your child. So come now, let your mother be with the man she loved, and let the past cease to pain you. The future awaits you—the birth of your child awaits you.'

She pressed her hands on theirs one last time and walked away, to speak a little to the priest.

Vito's arm came around Rachel again, and his hand rested on the swell on her abdomen. She leant her head against him.

'My mother has spoken the truth,' he said. 'We must let the past go, for it does not belong to us. Only the future belongs to us—and to our child. But—' his breath caught '—our happiness will be our gift to them all—and to our child. Our children.'

He kissed her gently, tenderly, his lips brushing the tears from her cheeks. A deep, abiding peace filled her.

'Oh, Vito—I love you so very much…'

He kissed her lips with soft reverence, his eyes lit with love.

'And I you. For all eternity.'

Together they turned and walked away from the past, and into the bright future that awaited them.

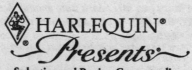

Coming Next Month

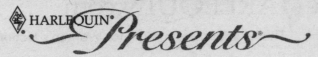

THE BEST HAS JUST GOTTEN BETTER!

#2481 BEDDING HIS VIRGIN MISTRESS Penny Jordan
Handsome billionaire Ricardo Salvatore is just as good at spending millions as he is at making them, and it's all for party planner Carly Carlisle. Rumor has it that the shy, and allegedly virginal, Carly is his mistress. But the critics say that Carly is just another woman after his cash....

#2482 IN THE RICH MAN'S WORLD Carol Marinelli
Budding reporter Amelia Jacobs has got an interview with billionaire Vaughan Mason. But Vaughan's not impressed by Amelia. He demands she spend a week with him, watching the master at work—the man whose ruthless tactics in the boardroom extend to the bedroom....

#2483 BOUGHT: ONE BRIDE Miranda Lee
Richard Crawford is rich, successful and thinking of his next acquisition—he wants a wife, but he doesn't want to fall in love. Holly Greenaway is the perfect candidate—a sweet, pretty florist with her livelihood in peril. Surely Richard can buy and possess her without letting his emotions get involved?

#2484 BLACKMAILED INTO MARRIAGE Lucy Monroe
Lia had rejected her aristocratic family, but now she needs their help. Their response is to sell her to the highest bidder, Damian Marquez, who wants Lia to provide him with an heir! As the wedding night looms, Lia knows the truth will out—she can't be his in the marriage bed....

#2485 THE SHEIKH'S CAPTIVE BRIDE Susan Stephens
After one passionate night, Lucy is the mother of Sheikh Kahlil's son, and if he is to inherit the kingdom of Abadan she must marry Kahlil! Lucy is both appalled by the idea of marrying the arrogant sheikh and overwhelmed by the attraction between them.

#2486 THE ITALIAN BOSS'S SECRET CHILD Trish Morey
At a masked ball, Damien DeLuca is swept away by a veiled beauty and the evening culminates in an explosive encounter. Philly Summers recognized her gorgeous Italian boss instantly—he's been invading her dreams for weeks. But she will keep her own identity secret!

HPCNM0705